THE DREAMSINGER

EDWARD MYERS

THE DREAMSINGER

EDWARD MYERS

MONTEMAYOR PRESS

MONTPELIER, VERMONT

FOR E.P.—

amica, sposa, musa

THE DREAMSINGER

EDWARD MYERS

[T]he whole universe is a symphony; in this every individual is one note, and his happiness lies in becoming perfectly attuned to the harmony of the universe.

—Hazrat Inayat Khan

[M]usical training is a more potent instrument than any other, because rhythm and harmony find their way into the inward places of the soul, on which they mightily fasten, imparting grace, and making the soul of him who is rightly educated graceful, or of him who is ill-educated ungraceful.

—Plato

I don't know what music is.

—Ludwig van Beethoven

Ned Jerosso, First Order Apprentice to the Lord High Builder of Instruments, made the last adjustments to his invention and, gazing upward, proclaimed it ready. A great pyramid of bird cages rose before him. Three times taller than a grown man, this device looked even stranger and more powerful than Ned had dared to hope. How could it fail to create astonishing music? How could it fail to impress the Masters? How could it fail to please even the Harmonor? Ned took a few steps and stared at his handiwork. Beyond the surge of confidence he now felt about his upcoming performance, Ned felt proud simply to have built such a remarkable instrument. He called it the avian calliope. It was his finest musical invention ever, and it would assure a triumph so complete as to make Ned's ascent inevitable. He felt no doubt that the Lord High Master of Masters would appoint him Assistant to the Lord High Builder of Instruments. In the fullness of time, Ned would surely find himself proclaimed the Lord High Builder. From that lofty place he might well become the next Master of Masters, second only in power to the Harmonor. Such would be the consequences of his new creation.

A twinge of concern disrupted his reverie. If Ned were to harvest the bounty he had struggled so hard to sow and cultivate, these birds needed to accomplish what he expected of them. Would they? That uncertainty—for these were, after all, wild creatures—prompted his only doubt.

Ned set to work checking the avian calliope yet again.

The bottom level of cages—stout boxes made of wire and wooden slats—housed the largest of the birds. Ned could see some of these creatures peering out: a red-crested crag dove, whose cry is low and mournful; an ice owl, whose hoot carries far from its mountain aerie; a pair of dawn-and-sunset birds, whose mating calls resemble the warble of a flute; and a young male swamp honker, whose warning cry is loud enough to knock the leaves off a tree. Other birds refused to reveal themselves, but Ned knew they lurked within their cages: a white-collared carrion-eater, two noon geese, a snowy hover bird, and even one of the rare stonefall wrens, whose warning call resembles the noise of rocks clacking and clattering as they tumble down a mountainside.

The next levels of the avian calliope, too, looked solid as a wall, each cage like a separate brick in the structure. Here Ned saw the variety of middle-sized birds he had selected: three cliff larks, a pair of night-flying fishers, a grave sentry, a couple of treetop roosters, a yellow-eyed shriek bird, a boulder hen, a frog-gulper, and even a wingless waddle bird. He could scarcely believe his luck in having assembled such a fine menagerie. Yet it wasn't what he saw that surprised him, remarkable as these birds looked, all those beaks poking through the wooden slats of the middle ranks of cages, and now and then golden crest feathers or bright red wings flashing through. No, it was how they would sing—how he hoped they would sing—that impressed Ned Jerosso.

Then the upper levels: the sight that exhilarated him most of all. Confined to the smallest, almost delicate cages forming the pyramid's summit were the rarest of all birds. Three starlight chasers. A cave denizen. Two honey suckers. A family of black-eyed hawks. A shadow bird. A smoky ember swallow. An array of birds whose melodies, once sung, would prompt even the Harmonor to weep with delight—

"Ready at last, I see."

Ned turned to see who spoke.

It was Sorrik, First-Order Emissary to the Lowlands. Few people could have so fully have reassured Ned at such a tense time. The old man's very presence felt calming: the warm smile eased Ned's worries, while Sorrik's appearance—the wise, weathered face, the white hair slanting from the sides of his head like clouds lingering near the summit of a bald mountaintop, and especially the snowy beard, which accumulated not so much on as under his chin—all these features soothed Ned's concerns.

Nothing, however, could put him fully at ease. "I hope it *is* ready," Ned muttered.

"It's a towering achievement in more ways than one," the old emissary said with a laugh.

"Spare me your wit."

"I offer my compliment with delight and admiration. It's most impressive."

"Assuming it works." When Ned gazed at the avian calliope, some of the birds stared back, unblinking, in anger and fear. Others, noisy but unseen, fidgeted within their cages. The whole contraption was so intricate!

"Of course it's going to work," Sorrik reassured him. "It's a beautiful sight."

"What worries me isn't how it looks."

"How it sounds, then? There, too, I see no cause for concerrn. You have chosen the birds that sing most sweetly, most powerfully."

"True—"

"What could possibly go wrong?"

Ned felt a twinge of panic. "Anything!" he blurted. "Everything!"

Sorrik huffed in amusement. "Come now."

"Sorrik, it's true. Never mind that the birds sing sweetly and powerfully—that's not all that matters. They must not just sing, but sing precisely when I command."

"As surely they will."

"Perhaps," Ned responded.

"You are a brilliant inventor of instruments," the old man assured him. "You are the most brilliant of all the apprentices currently among us."

Ned felt his anxieties fade like spring snow.

"The Lord High Builder has told me so himself."

So deep was Ned's embarrassment on hearing all this praise that he couldn't respond.

"Otherwise," Sorrik continued, "why would the Masters allow you to perform here today in the first place?"

"Well—"

"No other apprentice has been granted such a high honor in many years."

"Perhaps they couldn't find anyone else?"

"Oh, nonsense! The Lord High Builder chose you. Why? Because he values your abundant gifts."

"Nonsense indeed," Ned stated.

Sorrik glanced about, betraying a moment's nervousness, and he whispered, "My suggestion: don't insult those who trust you."

"All I meant—"

"Many Masters have expressed eagerness to hear what you have created," Sorrik went on, now in his normal voice, "and not just the Lord High Builder, I assure you."

"Truly?"

"Truly. The Masters of the Low and Middle Choirs. The Masters of the Middle and High Consorts—"

Ned felt a twinge of excitement about what would soon take place. If everything went well—

"There's even a rumor," said Sorrik, "that the Harmonor himself may appear."

"The Harmonor?" asked Ned, who fell silent in surprise and fear.

"The Harmonor."

Within a short time guests began to arrive. Members of the lowest ranks came first: the Low Choir and the Low Consort, the Low Apprentices to the various trades, and the Novice Song Guards. They filed in, each wearing their characteristic robes—each robe woven to show the colors and patterns signifying the wearers' ranks and roles as they took their seats on the stone benches that curved around the concert hall known as the Great Circle. Most of these guests were young, fifteen to twenty years old, and a few looked as if they had scarcely left childhood behind. The lads and the lasses alike wore long braids that dangled down their backs and swayed as they walked. Next came members of the Middle Choir and the Middle Consort, the Middle Apprentices, and others of their same rank. These members looked more varied in age—some youthful, some more mature—with the shapes of their bodies and the hue of their hair suggesting the differences in how long they had lived and worked within their orders. After them arrived the high ranks: Choir, Consort, and Apprenticeship, many of them older, grayer, and less agile than those preceding. Everyone proceeded quietly, calmly, and in perfect order. Soon the Masters arrived: Low, Middle, and High, almost all advanced in years and all accompanied by their attendants. They took their seats, too, until all the benches surrounding the Great Circle were completely filled.

Ned Jerosso observed all these people arriving and felt a mix of delight, excitement, and alarm. Everyone who mattered in Sifirithi had come to hear him!

Everyone except—

Where was the Harmonor?

Gazing about, Ned tried to spot him but couldn't. No Harmonor! Ned didn't know whether to laugh in relief or groan in despair. A great burden fell away from him, yet he felt deeply disappointed.

"Don't worry," said Sorrik as if reading Ned's mind. "He will hear of your great victory soon enough."

Ned couldn't even answer.

Soon all the guests were seated. Everyone waited, watching, as Ned got ready.

Ned looked around. Except for the Harmonor, not a single person of significance appeared to be missing. The tiers of seats rose all around him, leaving Ned alone with his huge instrument as if at the bottom of a valley. Beyond the Great Circle, the stone towers of Sifirithi rose toward the surrounding peaks until the man-made cliffs and the real ones—the ring of mountains—were indistinguishable. A light wind dipped down from the painfully blue sky, whistled against the cages, and ruffled the feathers of the birds.

He turned to the avian calliope and started to play.

From the very first note, the controls worked just as Ned had intended. Each lever pulled a cord, each cord tugged a mechanism in a cage, and each mechanism prompted a bird to sing. Sometimes this meant that a device of some sort prodded the bird until it squawked, hooted, yelled, or cheeped. At other times a device raised a baffle between two cages, revealing a predator to its prey, and prompting either or both birds to call out. At still other times the cord dangled a morsel of food before a bird, which then yelped in delight or hunger. In this manner, Ned coaxed all the birds to sing, whether separately or together, and a great swell of music rose from the calliope.

It works, he told himself. *It works exactly as I've intended.*

Melodies rose, took flight, and intertwined like swallows flipping about in mid-air on a summer evening. Even Ned felt shocked by the beauty of what he had created. When he glanced right or left at his audience, he saw undeniable signs that these people felt impressed, even moved, by what they heard.

Ned played confidently and elegantly. He couldn't have felt more delighted with himself or with what he had accomplished. Having invented such a mighty and subtle instrument, he would surely encounter no limit to what Ned could attain within Sifirithi, no limit to his power.

Just then something odd happened. What took place started with an event so insignificant that Ned ignored it at first: a bird landed on the calliope. An ordinary bird. A sparrow, perhaps—a small, drab female—who had flown in from elsewhere. Perhaps the music had attracted her. Alighting on the topmost cage, she roosted there, twitching, hopping about, trying to understand the commotion below. All the birds in the pyramid of cages ignored her; most were probably unaware of her presence. They continued to sing on cue. Great waves of melody rolled forth like surf. Ned glanced at the little newcomer now and then but otherwise paid no attention, so indifferent did he feel about her arrival. Let the sparrow roost up there if she wished! Let her listen! Well aware that the gathered citizens, the various choirs, and even the Masters themselves continued paying close attention to the concert, Ned played the avian calliope without the least worry that such a tiny change would affect the outcome.

Then the sparrow began to sing. Is "sing" the right word? Ned, listening to the first notes that came forth from her, asked himself that question at once. He felt as if he had done far more than simply listen to a plain little bird sing a song. He felt as if while half-starved, he had savored the first morsel of a feast. As if while dying of thirst, he had swallowed a mouthful of cold water. As if while lonely and bereft, he had felt the warmth of a friend's embrace. Against his will, Ned ceased to manipulate the avian calliope's controls. He stood, confused and motionless, before the instrument. He listened.

He wasn't alone in doing so. By now the caged birds had fallen silent. Somehow these creatures heard the tiny sparrow's liquid notes despite the racket of all their hoots, bellows, screeches, warbles, cries, moans, whoops, and wails; and, having heard the small bird's song, all the others now waited for a long, uncertain moment.

The human audience, too, listened. The gathered citizens. The Low Choir. The Middle Choir. The High and Middle Consorts. The Masters of all those groups. The Apprentices. The Lord High Builder of Instruments. All of them watched, waited, listened.

Then Ned heard the Lord High Builder's stern voice: "What is the meaning of this?"

At once great commotion erupted. An ice owl screeched, and its chilly cry, alarming to smaller birds, panicked the cliff larks. Fluttering desperately within their cages, the larks agitated the snowy hover bird right below them. The hover bird wailed only once but so loudly that the noise startled the noon geese. The geese in turn jostled hard inside their cage until its framework of slats and wire collapsed, freeing the geese and damaging that corner of the pyramid. Finding themselves abruptly freed, the geese took off at once and flew away. At the same instant, the treetop roosters in the cage above came crashing down, the cage shattered like a pumpkin, and the roosters escaped into the air. This noise in turn terrified the stonefall wrens, the waddle-birds, the grave sentry, the starlight chasers, and the cave denizen. Within little more than a moment that allowed Ned to blink in astonishment, the avian calliope started to collapse. The thrashing of so many birds weakened the bonds between the cages. Some of the doors fell open. Several cages split apart. Birds both large and small—predators and prey alike—took to the air. The crag dove attacked a boulder hen. The black-eyed hawk pursued a honey sucker. The night-flying fishers swooped, rose, and swooped again. The air churned with birds.

Ned, terrified, clasped his hands over his head to protect himself and stared in astonishment as the avian calliope fell to pieces, releasing the captive creatures, crumbling, and letting pieces of wood, metal, and fragments of cages topple toward the audience.

"Get away!" a man yelled.

"Run for your lives!" a woman shouted.

Even before these warnings rang out, people had begun to flee. Some backed off. Others turned and sprinted away. So crowded was the Great Circle, however, that few could escape without slamming into others. People sought safety as well as possible, but many, desperate to escape, tripped and fell. Others toppled over them. Still others stumbled on fallen bodies.

Cries of injury and fear soon overwhelmed even the racket of all the panic-stricken birds wheeling overhead.

Ned, scarcely able to stay upright, surveyed the chaos surrounding him. People dashed every which way. The Lord High Builder tripped on a broken cage and fell. Two members of the Low Choir huddled together on the ground. A Middle Choir Master wept and hollered, his face streaked with blood. Three children from the Low Choir cried out for their mothers.

It seemed impossible that so much could have gone so wrong.

The avian calliope lay before him, cages scattered everywhere. All the birds had fled.

Except one.

At first Ned nearly missed her, she was so small. When something caught his eye, however—a twitch somewhere on a cage—he realized that the little sparrow hadn't left. She roosted just a few arm lengths away. Looking this way and that, the bird didn't seem scared, only puzzled by all the commotion. Then she turned slightly and stared right at Ned.

He felt so bewildered to see of all his work reduced to rubble that he couldn't even speak.

The bird stared at Ned for a moment, then sprang into the air and flew away.

1

THE DREAMSONGS

1

Imagine, if you will, a land empty of all music. A land in which the people have no songs to sing, no tunes to play, no jigs to start them dancing. A land in which music isn't just absent, but forbidden.

At the time of a baby's birth, no songs of jubilation fill the air. Later, as the child grows, no nursery rhymes or jump-rope tunes accompany her play. When she reaches womanhood and marries, no wedding hymns celebrate the bond she's making with her husband, and there's no dancing at the festivities because no singers sing and no players play. At the birth of her own child, the mother sings no lullabies to calm the babe. Neither does she sing in joy, contentment, delight, or lamentation as the years pass. And when she dies, no one plays a dirge at her funeral.

What you have imagined is a land that existed not so long ago—the Realm of Siir—and although you may know nothing of such a place, it existed all the same. I know this claim to be true, for I visited Siir myself many times. Not just visited: I served the Masters who ruled over that silent realm.

Which prompts me to change the words I spoke earlier . . .

It's not altogether true that Siir was *empty* of music. There was music. But the people of Siir had no music of their own. The distant rulers in a city called Sifirithi had banned singing, playing, and making of music by any means other than their own, and, like a king demanding payment from his subjects in cattle, wheat, or gold, the Masters of Sifirithi had hoarded all music to serve their purposes. Those purposes differed greatly from what suited the people they ruled. In fact, the Masters of Sifirithi used music as a means to dominate everyone in Siir. This is why music was forbidden.

Thus although the people of Siir had once made their own music, they had lost that privilege many years ago. Two generations had grown up with no memory of music. They had never heard a lullaby, a harvest tune, or a solstice hymn. They had never owned or played a musical instrument of any kind. They had never sung even the simplest melody. Indeed, music might as well never have existed. Of course a few people, most of them very old, could remember how to sing, but they knew better than to let even a single note pass their lips. A small number of other old men and women could play instruments—what had once been called lutes, fiddles, flutes, harps, drums, and horns—but the Masters had confiscated or destroyed all instruments long ago, and none of the players would have risked playing anyway. Besides, no one would have dared to listen. Listening would have been too risky, itself an afront to the Masters and a violation of their laws.

When travelers from faraway lands passed through Siir and noticed the silence, they asked, "What, are you all mute?" or "Doesn't anyone here sing but the birds?" The people of Siir only laughed and changed the subject. They knew enough about their silence already; no one needed to say more. If a nosy traveler kept asking, someone would nervously reply, "What, shall we make music out of thin air?" or "A thirsty man wants water, but thirst alone won't let him drink."

The town of Laro was like the rest of Siir, and a girl named Allu was like everyone else in Laro—at least until she was twelve years old. Living with her family in a small thatch-roofed cottage, Allu possessed no abilities nor performed any duties different from any other girl her age. She helped her parents by doing chores. She played each day when finished with her tasks. She enjoyed the company of a few friends. She was altogether ordinary.

Then the dreamsongs began.

Lying in bed one night, Allu heard voices in the dark. Not just one voice, but many. Men, women, children: they called out in ways that Allu had never imagined before, much less heard. The song came from everywhere and nowhere. Baffled, Allu listened for a long time without moving from her bed.

> I'll sail the sea in a boat made of water—
> Spray my canvas, bubbles my keel—
> I'll put back the fish that fishermen slaughter
> With a net, a trap, a line, and a reel.

She didn't know where this song came from or what it meant. She knew only that it stirred some kind of deep longing within her and gave her a satisfaction that she couldn't explain or identify. She knew as well that this song was forbidden.

> I'll furrow the fields with an artichoke thorn,
> Sow the soil with shadows and snow—
> I'll harvest the darkness like cabbage and corn
> As icicles hiss in the earth as they grow.

Why, then, would people have sung it? Who would have risked their lives so foolishly? She didn't know. She knew only that singing such a song, even listening to it, was dangerous beyond all reckoning.

> I'll sing you a song without words or a tune—
> My tongue is silent, my voice is mute—
> I'll play you music on a tree in bloom:
> Bees the melody, blossoms the lute.

Allu jumped out of bed, rushed to the window, flung open the shutters, and glanced about. The muddy lane below her window, the stone cottages huddled opposite, the thatched roofs blotting great masses from the starry sky—were silent. The cottages were dark. The lane was empty. Allu stood there a long moment, listening, before she closed the shutters and returned to bed.

The next morning, at breakfast, Allu said, "That was so strange."

"What was?" asked her mother as she and Allu's father worked at the hearth. Two small copper kettles flanked a larger one over the flames. Steam and rich aromas wafted from all three pots.

"Those people singing last night."

Both Allu's mother and father ignored her. One of her two sisters laughed with clear discomfort; her brother only stared.

Allu said, "It's true—some people sang. Didn't you hear them?"

"You must have been dreaming," said Mother.

"No, I heard them."

"You heard them in a dream." Father carried some food to the family—the gray boiled grain that would be their only meal until suppertime—and he served everyone qucikly, almost abruptly. "Now eat. We have a hard day's work ahead."

The older sister, Satifa, said, "You didn't hear anything."

"I did!" Allu insisted.

"Why should you hear what the rest of us haven't?" asked the younger sister, Lálasa.

"I don't know, but I did!"

Allu's father, an ironsmith who was ordinarily silent, patient, and kind, said, "Enough! Let's not squabble like a pen full of turkeys."

Allu told him, "I heard the music. People sang to me."

"It was a dream," said Mother. "Not a good dream, either. Listen to me: there will be no more talk of singers in the night."

That occasion was only the first that Allu mentioned to her family. Within a few days, others followed. She didn't want to talk about the dreamsongs, but she did anyway, and on each occasion Father told her to stop, her sisters and brother teased her, and Mother pleaded with Allu not to utter this alarming nonsense. They had no time to waste on such foolishness. Life in Laro was hard enough, dangerous enough, already.

Their responses made no difference. The dreamsongs kept coming.

Allu herself grew comfortable with them. She soon looked forward to their arrival. Every few days, strange voices reached her while she slept. The dreamsongs most often started softly, grew louder, and faded. At other times they arrived more suddenly, like a gust of wind that left Allu shaking. She sat upright in bed, clutched her blanket, and looked every which way. She never saw anything and never heard a sound but Father's snores, Mother's sighs, and the ticking embers in the hearth, yet Allu never doubted that something had come to her. She welcomed the voices and the music they brought.

2

That autumn, while helping her parents with the harvest, Allu stood waist-deep in the family's wheatfield. Wind rushed and rustled over the ripe grain, swirling and whirling, alternately smoothing and roughening the great radiant expanse, and a complex murmur rose from the intermingling of air and wheat. Allu, her parents, her sisters, and her brother worked together in a line, each wielding a sickle to reap handfuls of the brittle stalks. Like the wind, the reaping made a rhythmic, almost musical noise, and birds leaped out of the field—pheasants, quail, grouse, crows—each with its own cry of alarm and warning as the harvesters advanced. Though working hard, Allu watched and listened, aware at some point that of all the living creatures present, only she and her family were silent.

"Why can't we sing?" she asked Mother during one of their brief rests.

Mother turned toward Allu suddenly, then glanced around. "Because it's forbidden," she answered at once. "Now let's get back to work."

"But why is it forbidden?"

"The day is late." Mother picked up her tools, stood, and walked off.

Allu rushed to catch up. "Why, Mother?"

Looking tired, Mother didn't even turn as she spoke. "Because the Masters deem it so."

"The Masters?"

"Enough questions, Allu. Who knows how far even your small voice carries."

"Mother—"

"Enough!"

≈ ≈ ≈

One day Allu ran a quick errand to the village marketplace. It was an ordinary errand on an ordinary day. Her parents simply needed a few items they had forgotten to buy earlier: two pennyweights of rye, three turnips, and a soup weasel. Allu felt pleased to leave the family cottage for a while. She had wearied of her endless chores that day, and she always enjoyed going to the marketplace. Because Allu often forgot the purpose of such errands, however, Allu's older sister, Satifa, came along to remind her.

"Don't tarry," Mother said as the girls left. "Stay out of trouble."

Allu and Satifa did as they were told. They visited the marketplace. They purchased the rye, the turnips, and the weasel. They started home.

What happened next was the strangest experience of Allu's life until that day. Two foreigners, and man and a woman, had ventured into town. Their brightly colored robes and unfamiliar accents marked them as newcomers not just to Laro but also to the whole Realm of Siir. What they proceeded to do, however, proved even stranger than how they looked.

The man sat with a bizarre object resting on his lap—an object about the size and shape of the handlooms that local folk used for weaving caps and kerchiefs—and this object appeared loom-like, too, because of the strings, fifteen or twenty in number, running side by side within its frame. Yet even a single glance revealed that this man wasn't weaving. He plucked at the strings as if removing lint from a loom's warp, but it lint wasn't what he brought away. It was sound. Strange, puzzling sound: clear and bright as newly dyed yarn. While the man plucked at this sound-loom, weaving a tapestry that Allu didn't see but heard, the woman sewed her own audible thread, too, calling out with her own voice in noises that interwove with the man's fabric seamlessly.

Allu watched and listened. She tried to make sense of what she saw and heard. Witnessing these two foreigners make odd sounds stirred Allu in some way that she couldn't identify—made her breathe faster, made her tremble and shiver—yet at the same time the very oddness, the pointlessness of their actions, prompted her to laugh. What were they doing? Why would anyone make such noises? She could tell that other villagers found these two people at least as strange as Allu herself did. Shopkeepers stared. Farmwives pointed and whispered to one another. Children raced around frantically or else gawked in silence.

Listening hard, Allu realized that words lay entangled in the woman's strand of sound:

> Listen to a song about the Realm of Siir,
> A land where none but the birds may sing.
> Listen to a song full of woe and fear—

Then, as if everyone suddenly woke from a dream, the villagers glanced at one another, called out in dismay, and backed off. The farmwives scurried away, clutching their baskets. The shopkeepers retreated to their shops. The children either fled with their parents or else lingered, staring, until the parents returned, grabbing the stubborn boys and girls and tugging them to safety. Within the span of a few heartbeats, everyone had disappeared.

Everyone, that is, but Allu, Satifa, and the two foreigners. Allu stood there, still watching. The foreigners, now silent, stared back. Startled by everyone's departure, one of the foreigners—the man— asked, "Is everyone here always in such a hurry?"

Allu felt Satifa tugging at her sleeve. "Allu, please!" cried the other girl. "We can't listen! We mustn't!"

The foreign woman laughed. "What, a little song will scare you off? Don't tell me you're afraid of music!"

"Don't even say the word!" Satifa exclaimed. Then she caught hold of Allu by the arm, yanked hard, and pulled her stumbling toward home.

Four winters came and went. Four springs blossomed. During that time, Allu changed from a girl into a young woman. Her duties, too, changed from those given to a child into those demanded from an adult. Allu did what she could to meet these demands. She took on tasks in the ironware shop. She helped her parents, sisters, and brother do household chores. She assisted in caring for the family's goats and chickens. Yet her parents despaired of their youngest daughter. Couldn't she master even the simplest tasks? She always seemed to be stumbling, breaking dishes and crockery, dipping her braids into the milk pail, or dropping food into the hearth. She grew more strange and awkward, not more graceful, with the passage of time. Plain in appearance, with messy brown hair and untidy clothes, she often looked like a forest creature that her parents had caught somewhere in the woods and brought home but hadn't fully tamed. She walked with an impatient stride and tripped a lot. The other children had already proved themselves useful. Allu? Not yet. Something else about her, too, troubled her parents. An oddness. An otherness. Even while sitting with everyone else in her family's small, smoky cottage, she seemed far away and alone.

What worried them most about Allu was the girl's persistence in asking questions that shouldn't have concerned her in the first place.

"Why have the Masters forbidden us to sing?" Allu asked Father one day when she visited him at his shop. He was standing near the furnace just then, pounding out a yellow-glowing iron rod on the anvil. The roar of the furnace and the clang of his hammer prevented him from hearing the words. Raising her voice, she repeated, "Why have the Masters forbidden us to sing?"

He stopped short, his hammer suspended in mid-air. He turned to Allu. Then he set down the hammer, strode over to the door, shut and bolted it, then closed all the windows.

Walking back to where she stood, Father gently grasped her shoulders. "Please, Allu, why do you insist on this foolishness?"

"I just want to know—"

"You have no good reason to ask."

"Father—"

"Listen," he said, speaking almost too softly for Allu to understand him. "All music belongs to the Masters. They own it. They do with it what they wish. If you sing, you steal what belongs to them."

"How does singing a song steal it—"

"That's not ours to decide. Only the Masters decide."

"Father—"

"Believe me, taking what belongs to the Masters will bring down their wrath on you, our family, and all of Laro."

She didn't believe them. The warnings made no sense. Who were the Masters, anyway? How could they claim to own what belonged to Allu (or to anyone else) as surely as the doves, the shrikes, and the meadow larks owned their spontaneous cries? Allu felt confident that all this spooky talk was nothing but village superstition.

Then, while walking near the edge of Laro one afternoon, Allu heard a peculiar sound. At first she thought it might have been a beast's bellowing: loud, painful, harsh. Perhaps a farmer was slaughtering a calf. Allu faltered, then continued on her way home. Her mother had sent her to buy spices at a neighboring village; having made the purchase, Allu didn't want to delay returning. The slaughter of a calf was no reason to be late.

Allu hesitated again. The sound rose and fell, rose again, wavering. Allu listened, uncomfortable at hearing such an unpleasant noise yet unable to break away. Something about it troubled her. Was this really a beast she heard, or perhaps a person?

She walked a few more paces, left the path, and waded into the field on her right. The stand of oats parted, then closed around her. Allu strode through the hissing oats.

There: ahead. A ramshackle hut and a man beside it.

Rassai the Fool, she told herself. Allu had heard of him over the years; she had even spotted him once or twice. Dressed in rags, smeared with dirt and soot, he was a man of about her parents' age whose disheveled state made him look far older. His appearance wasn't what caught Allu's attention now. It wasn't even the noise he made—his voice rising, falling, wavering—a noise that both frightened her and drew her forth. Something else made Allu crouch, hide herself among the oats, watch, and listen.

I hate the Masters!
I hate their songs!
I hate their instruments!
I hate their melodies!
I hate their guts!

Six other people had approached the Fool's hut. Dressed in robes of gray, white, and red cloth, they could have been either men or women, but Allu couldn't tell which because of their attire and the distance between them and herself. She had never seen these people or anyone like them. Now they stood before Rassai while he ranted. To Allu's surprise, these robed strangers called back to him: called back not in words, but in other sounds that their voices made. Sounds that made no sense. Sounds that said something and did something despite their senselessness. Rassai the Fool ranted. The strangers chanted. Little by little, the Fool's ranting diminished. His angry squeal subsided. His voice fell silent. The strangers' chanting calmed, subdued, and rendered the Fool as gentle and calm as a sleepy old dog.

Allu watched from her hiding place. She felt so afraid that she wanted to run away, yet so afraid that she couldn't move.

All the more so when the strangers surrounded Rassai the Fool, tied his hands, and, fastening a rope to his wrists, led him away like a calf destined for the marketplace.

3

Soon after that, something else happened. Not only did Allu keep hearing voices; she also discovered her own.

Allu could remember singing as a little girl, singing as all children sing—even if only skip-rope songs and little tunes for calling out to friends—and she could recall her parents scolding or teasing her until the singing stopped. "No, you mustn't sing!" Mother had told her time after time. "Never sing at all!" She could recall Father teasing her: "Who do you think you are, a nightingale?" As she grew older, Allu's parents had explained why there must be no singing: "Don't do what the Masters have forbidden, or they'll come and take you away." Having seen what had happened to Rassai the Fool, she now believed these warnings, and she feared that they might come true.

Yet she sang anyway. Allu sang because the dreamsongs came to her, the voices called out, and they roused something within her. Allu called back, singing songs that rose unexpectedly from within, just as frightened meadowlarks rise from a wheatfield as the harvesters approach with their sickles and scythes.

And when she sang, the villagers in Laro stopped to listen. People filling buckets at the well stepped away from the water's splash and slosh to hear better. Smiths, cobblers, and carpenters at work somehow took notice despite their own noise, then held off a moment to pay attention. Even the children playing street games looked around as Allu's unexpected, unwelcome melodies drifted through Laro. Then everyone slammed doors, shut windows, or rushed off, already afraid.

Allu, cooking dinner one spring afternoon, sang idly to herself as she stirred the pots.

> Go to bed, my mother said—
> The wind's in the leaves
> And the rain's on the pane.
> We'll harvest the sheaves,
> We'll winnow the grain,
> We'll bake the bread
> In the morning.

"Stop!" Mother shouted.

"Stop *what?*" asked Allu, suddenly aware of her surroundings. Her whole family was staring at her.

"You know what."

"I'm not harming anyone," Allu protested.

"No? Wait till the Masters find out."

"It's just a song."

"Just a song! Even if that were true, what good is it? Can a song churn butter? Can a song hammer iron? Peel potatoes? Run errands? You should work at your tasks instead of chirping."

"It's not just chirping—"

Mother imitated Allu in a high, squeaky voice. Allu's brother and sisters joined in, laughing nervously.

Allu watched and listened to them. She said nothing to defend herself. So much laughter in a small room made her dizzy. She would have gone outside, but that would have turned everyone's amusement into anger, since dinner was already late. All she could do was stay there at the hearth. Allu stirred a pot on the fire and ignored everyone around her. It was easier than she thought: the voices came to her then, as they did more and more often, out of nowhere, even while she was awake; she listened, now content, to the clear melody; and, without even trying, she found her own voice joining those she heard.

> We'll bake the bread
> In the morning.

"*Stop!*" Mother shouted once again.

Allu fell silent. Looking at her, she saw something different from what she expected in her mother's face: not rage, but fear.

"Allu, Allu—don't you understand?" She stepped closer, arms open. She took Allu in her embrace. "This isn't just our own safety that concerns us. It's yours as well."

"I'm not hurting anyone," she said, convinced that what she said was true. This wasn't like Rassai the Fool's ranting. "It's just a song."

"What if the Masters in Sifirithi learn you're singing 'just a song'?"

Father interrupted, "They already have."

Allu turned to him. She saw Mother look at him, too, her face suddenly pale.

"Today an emissary from Sifirithi came to Laro," he continued. "He asked around, located the shop, and visited me there."

Allu's mother sat abruptly as if to avoid fainting. "Just as I feared."

"He spoke to me. I listened. He granted me time to doubt him, question him, and think a while."

"So what does he want!"

Allu was frantic with curiosity now—curiosity and alarm.

"What he wants," said Father, "is the girl. He knows of her—of her voice, her singing. The Masters know of her. The Masters in Sifirithi." He glanced at Allu, then at his wife.

Mother said, "I knew it!"

"They want her."

"Because of the singing?"

Allu felt sick. At once she remembered the sight of Rassai the Fool, bound with rope and led away. She staggered forth, unsure of her footing, bumped into a bench, and sat beside her mother.

"Because of the singing," said Father.

Allu listened without understanding the words. Sifirithi . . . They were speaking of the place to which people are taken and from which they never return.

"What did you tell him, then?" Mother asked.

"I told him to leave."

Allu felt a great sense of relief. Surely Father would protect her.

"Told him to leave!" exclaimed Mother, sounding shocked. "The Masters sent an emissary—and you told him to leave? As if we're not in enough trouble already?"

Father slumped forward, resting his face in his hands. For a moment he sat motionless; then Allu saw his shoulders shaking as he sobbed. Without looking up he said, "I told him to leave and then come back at a better time. The girl was out milking the goats. I promised him we'll have her ready tomorrow."

Allu jerked upright as if doused her cold water. *Ready tomorrow.* She said, "Father—?" but fell silent.

"I'm sorry," he replied, his expression empty with grief. "Please forgive me."

Allu didn't know what to say.

Her mother, sisters, and brother simply stared at one another. Mother began to weep.

"What should I have done?" asked Father. "Should I have refused him? Insulted him? What would have come of it? The emissary would have our entire family hauled off to Sifirithi."

"But Father——" Dizzy, Allu clung to the bench for support.

"I'm so, so sorry."

She wished someone would come close and comfort her, but no one moved. Didn't they love her? Or were they simply too afraid to show her any love?

Father gestured helplessly with both hands. "Please forgive me."

4

She left in a box-like coach that ten brawny young men lifted and carried as Allu's family, a few neighbors, and some other towns-people saw her off.

Allu watched them in a daze of bewilderment and fear. How could her parents let this happen? Why didn't someone try to rescue her? She didn't expect much from the villagers—they would strive only to save themselves—but Allu felt furious anyway. No one did anything to help. People only stared. Perhaps they felt bewildered that a villager should leave in such splendor, for the coach was lovely, built of dark, polished wood and finely woven cloth, and the ten men shouldering it wore intricately embroidered robes. Even so, Allu felt outraged by the villagers' indifference. Indifference—or cowardice? Either way, it seemed that she had already ceased to exist. She was already dead, buried, and forgotten.

Allu ignored them. Fighting back tears, she turned from the sight of the villagers and waited for the coach to leave. The emissary, a black-robed old man with soft white hair and a wispy beard, smiled at her from where he sat on the opposite seat. She couldn't understand his friendliness. If he was taking her away to Sifirithi, why did he smile with such warmth? She averted her gaze from the old man too.

Glancing outside again, Allu caught sight of her family. Her parents held each other as if incapable of staying upright without assistance. One of her sisters kept glancing about, the other pressed her head against Mother's skirt, and Allu's brother simply stared at the ground. None of them appeared to see her. Allu realized just then that, isolated by their sadness, her family was already far, far away.

The head carrier cried out, the coach rose and shifted, and they set off.

Allu gazed blankly as the countryside around her unfolded. Fields, meadows, farms, and woods eased by. She recognized a few of the villages: Sarruffa, Chosto, Lentu-on-the-Forro. . . Others looked unfamiliar. In just half a morning, Allu went farther than she had ever gone before in her life. The coach wound its way among the hills. Settlements passed without Allu understanding where she was. Dogs followed, barking. Boys shouted. All this noise and the constant motion confused Allu, and it alarmed her, too, for passing each town, hillside, farm, and crossroads put Laro still more distant, Sifirithi closer and closer.

Sifirithi, Allu thought. The Masters' city.

The emissary and Allu proceeded for most of a day. They stopped now and then, let the carriers rest, and bought a meal from one of the roadside inns.

"Here," said the emissary, offering Allu a bowl of sparrow soup.

She shook her head.

"You must eat," said the emissary. "You must maintain your strength."

Again she shook her head. She felt too frightened to feel hungry.

Only the newness of what she saw kept her from despair. The houses looked different: tile or wooden roofs instead of thatch. People dressed in strange clothes: fur robes and elaborate leather caps. Even the air seemed unfamiliar: light, cool, soft to the touch. Afternoon sunbeams shot through the rows of trees and striped the road. Shadows fell over Allu, cold as water.

"Sir?" she inquired.

"My name is Sorrik-koru," said the emissary.

"Yes, sir."

"Please call me Sorrik."

"How much longer until we arrive?"

Sorrik smiled his inexplicably kind smile again.

"It will not be long."

Soon the coach began climbing even more steeply than before. The carriers struggled slowly up a hillside by angling first to the right, then to the left, then to the right again, back and forth, pausing often but making good progress. Allu could see a huge valley spread out below. Forests covered the land; villages dotted the forests. Smoke rose here and there, and the sound of someone chopping wood came to her faintly. The sun set. Dusk deepened. Allu, now tired, fell asleep under a blanket that Sorrik spread over her. She awoke now and then, unsure what was happening, sometimes afraid; then she remembered, reminded herself, settled in, and dozed off again . . .

Half-asleep, Allu remembered the day before. She had sung for this emissary, Sorrik. He had listened, smiling at her while she sang, and he had told Allu's parents, "She is welcome in Sifirithi. There will be a place for Allu in the Choir."

"Singing is forbidden," said Mother.

"Not in Sifirithi. Not in the Choir." He explained the arrangement and the terms. Then he left. Allu's parents, he said, should have a while to think things over.

Allu herself scarcely knew what to believe. She knew that no one would listen to her opinions, yet she couldn't restrain her thoughts any more than she restrained the voices that came to her. It surprised her as much as her family that someone—anyone!—would travel a great distance just to hear a young villager sing her songs.

She loved singing; she sang as much as possible. She had even sung for this lean, pale stranger in his fine black robe, and she felt happy that he liked her singing. But this made no sense. Just as Allu didn't choose the air she breathed, she didn't choose the melodies she sang. What happened simply happened. Even so, the emissary liked her singing. What amazed her was that singing might prompt something other than punishment.

Or would it?

That last night in Laro, while Allu pretended to lie sleep in bed, she had listened to her parents.

"—but I worry about the consequences," Mother had said. "After all, it won't be a mere village. It will be Sifirithi."

Sifirithi! The city's name filled any villager with bafflement and dread.

Father asked, "What choice have we?"

Mother fell silent for a while. "Our own daughter!"

"Think of it as an offering," said Father. "We pour wine as an offering to the gods in hopes they'll spare us any hardships. So with the Masters in Sifirithi. Perhaps they will spare us for having offered Allu so freely."

Mother said, "You make it sound as if it's all decided."

"Think of what will happen if we refuse."

Now she too fell silent.

Father said, "I feel sure they will not harm her. Who knows? Perhaps she will thrive in Sifirithi. The emissary promised that the girl won't suffer."

"But to tear a child from her family!"

"She has never been happy here. She's a lark in a henhouse. Let her go to where she can do us some good."

"And the child? What of her?"

"As much as we love Allu," said Father, "we can't risk the fate of our whole family—of the whole village—on her account. We simply have to hope they'll treat her well."

Allu awoke with a jolt. She felt confused for a moment; then she remembered the coach, the carriers, the emissary, and the long ride. Brilliant orange light now streamed through the windows. Allu shielded her eyes. Despite the dazzle, however, she shook from the cold. Even the blanket she clutched around her didn't help. Allu glanced up at Sorrik. Still seated across from her, the thin little man motioned for Allu to look outside.

"Where are we?" she asked, leaning over to the window. All she could see was the sunrise—yellow above and orange below, radiant—nothing but light.

Sorrik told her, "We're almost there. Now if you wait a moment—
there! Look again," he said, and he pointed suddenly.

Allu saw at once that the coach, bumping along, followed the
mountainside, its path little more than a long, narrow shelf cut into
the slope. A rock wall rose to one side, a cliff fell away on the other,
and ahead, still at a distance, shapeless in the glare, a city spread out
in the curve between two peaks. Allu stared without moving. The light
almost blinded her, yet she was unable to turn away. She could hardly
tell where the city ended and the sunrise began.

"Sifirithi," she said. "Sifirithi."

II

THE VIEW FROM NED'S WORKSHOP

5

Standing at the largest of his windows, Ned Jerosso gazed at Sifirithi spread out below. His workshop jutted out from a building located halfway up the mountainside and thus allowed him a nearly full view of the city, a view that had delighted him throughout his six years of living and working in these rooms but that now, given the recent fiasco, felt like mockery. Ned could see the several town squares and the squat stone buildings of the complex city. He could see the network of alleyways and streets that ordinarily bustled with men, women, and children but now, well before dawn, looked almost empty. He could see the center of Sifirithi, the Great Circle that functioned as the heart of this vibrant organism and that pumped a constant flow of people through the city's arteries and veins. The heart was still, the lifeblood absent.

He couldn't tolerate the sight for long, so he pulled away and stepped back into his workshop. His lair. The place where he spent his wakeful and sleeping hours alike. The setting for his most creative efforts and for the fatigue that these efforts now induced in him. The laboratory where Ned took dead materials—wood, brass, copper, glass, wire, feathers, string, stone—and transmuted them through processes that Ned himself still didn't fully understand into devices that somehow came alive, moved, spoke, and sang. This workshop had been the site of Ned's greatest exhilaration, his greatest hopes. Had been. And was no longer.

"I'm sorry, Master," Ned had told Atalessi, the Lord High Builder of Instruments, four days earlier, shortly after the calamity in the Great Circle.

The Master, attired in his black-and-scarlet robe while seated at his workbench, had simply nodded. His dark beard and full mustache made it difficult for Ned to see the Master's mouth, hence also difficult to detect a smile or a frown there. With only the man's eyes visible, he often looked like someone peering through a hedge.

Ned assumed there was no smile. "I did my best," he explained.

Another nod.

"Unfortunately, the design contained certain—limitations."

No response.

For a long time Ned simply stood there, gazing at the Lord High Builder and, when his Master stayed silent, Ned looked around at the huge workshop: the multitude of tools on racks; the stacks of lumber, sheet metal, animal hide, fabric, bone, glass, stone, and other materials; the dozens of musical instruments dangling from the rafters on cords, resting on shelves, or waiting, untouched and silent, on the floor. Ned had spent many hours each day over the past six years in this room, where he had watched the Master, listened to him, and followed his instructions. Talkative by nature and enthusiastic about his craft, the Lord High Builder had never lacked for words in the past. Ned, facing his silence now, couldn't have felt more fully reprimanded if the Master had battered him with curses.

"Master—"

Another nod.

"Please believe me, Master: I am deeply sorry."

Now the Lord High Builder turned in his chair and faced Ned for the first time. "Listen to me closely, Ned Jerosso," he replied. "You are the most gifted apprentice I have allowed to work with me. Ever. You are, in fact, the most gifted young practitioner of this art that anyone among the Masters can remember. For these reasons, you can imagine why the other day's event so deeply disturbs me."

"Master—"

The High Builder raised his hand to silence Ned. "It's not as if you're an untutored novice. I've been teaching you for years, Ned. *Years.* Who would imagine that after so much training, you—you, of all people!—would subject yourself to such humiliation. And, I might add, subject me as well."

Ned felt the urge to apologize again but held off. "I'll resign," he said abruptly.

"Ned—"

"In fact, I resign."

"Ned, listen to me."

"I resign right now."

Ned wasn't bluffing. Ashamed and sad, he saw no recourse but to end what had clearly been a mistake. His apprenticeship had been misbegotten from the start. Ned should no longer be an apprentice inventing and building instruments, he told himself—he should be a servant boy sweeping floors, lugging water, and shoveling the ashes out of dirty hearths.

As Ned turned to leave, however, the High Builder stood abruptly, reached out, and grasped him by the arm. "Stop. I won't allow you such a quick escape," he stated calmly. "Nothing so easy as that. No— you must redeem yourself."

Ned, hearing these words, resisted at first, then clung to them as if to a branch providing his only handhold as he dangled from a cliff. "Redeem myself," he said, not quite believing the words. "How would I do that, Master? How can I undo what I've done? Tell me."

The High Builder said nothing at first. Neither smiling nor frowning, he merely gazed at his apprentice. "I haven't decided yet," he told Ned.

How was it possible that he could have fallen so low? Never mind his workshop's lofty placement halfway up the mountain. Ned couldn't help but imagine all the people down in the city looking toward his window and, turning to someone nearby, saying, "Look, there's Ned Jerosso's workshop! Did you hear what happened?" or: "I'm so glad I wasn't at his concert!" or: "Small wonder the lad is hiding—I, too, would be scared to show my face after what took place the other day!"

What pained Ned more than the sharp comments that assailants surely shot toward him now was how richly he deserved to be the target of their darts and arrows. Avian calliope, indeed! Had any-one ever devised a more preposterous musical instrument? If he had striven with all his skill to humiliate himself—and, simultaneously, to annoy, alarm, exasperate, and infuriate the Masters—he couldn't have accomplished his goal much more thoroughly by intention than he had by accident. Looking back on his concert, Ned felt surprised only that the occasion hadn't resulted in more injuries, perhaps even a death or two. Ned's neck and face prickled at the recollection; his brow grew damp. How the birds had grown unruly . . . How they had shrieked, cawed, hooted, moaned, and whistled . . . How they had sprung into the air . . . How they had flown back and forth when their cages fell to the ground and split open . . . How the audience, panicking, had screamed and wailed . . . Concert indeed!

In his worst nightmares Ned had never dreamed of such an awful outcome to his quest. He had been constructing musical instruments since before even fully understanding what they were. His parents, watching him drum on the tabletop as a toddler and clink his spoon against a cup as a little boy, had, as he grew older, given him materials instead of toys to play with: pieces of wood, shells, beads, strings and strands, little boxes, strips of leather, smooth sheets of hammered brass and copper. Before the start of his seventh year, Ned had known he possessed a gift for assembling such things in new ways and coaxing music out of them. He hadn't been the only one who saw his gift. His mother and father had, too, and they had delighted in their son's abilities. They had made sure that the Masters perceived it as well: they had taken Ned, age eight, to Arisávala, the Low Builder of Instruments, and showed her what their son had accomplished without any guidance beyond what his parents' enthusiasm had provided. Within a few days the boy had started receiving private instruction from the Low Builder herself. By age ten he had become a Third-Order Apprentice to the Middle Builder. Before the end of that same year, he had ascended to the status of First-Order Apprentice—the youngest in anyone's memory to attain that rank. Ned's ascent continued at a pace that would have caused puzzlement and consternation within Sifirithi had the fruit of his apprenticeship not yielded such a lush harvest: scores of instruments between the start of his training and, four years later, his appointment as First Order Apprentice to the Lord High Builder of Instruments.

Now, convinced that his career had ended before he had reached his eighteenth year, Ned wandered through his workshop, surveyed the benches and the racks, and gazed at some of his past and present creations. A tiny xylophone made from the wing bones of a bat. A drum made from an antelope's skull. A string of bells, each as small as a kernel of wheat, fashioned from the dried-out bladders of mice. Glass flutes. Harps of all sizes. Windchimes. He played some of them, each briefly and without much interest. Music hid inside these instruments. Until just four days ago, the instruments and the music that Ned coaxed out of them would have inspired delight. They had been both the goal of his quest and the path for reaching that goal. They had been Ned's best and most personal contribution to the Realm. He had worked hard to create the most powerful instruments—worked hard not just to pursue this quest in its own right, but to help foster harmony throughout the Realm. Now each of these devices seemed a pointless joke. Each reminded him that Ned had not only failed to reach his goal: he would never reach it. Ever.

Small wonder that so many people throughout Sifirithi now avoided him. Few would even speak with him. Not that Ned really blamed them; the danger was too great. Like fresh fruit stored in the same box as a tainted apple, what started out pure might well begin to rot by touching what was impure. Why would anyone risk contact with Ned? Nobody would be so reckless.

Well, almost none. Only Sorrik, Ned's oldest friend, had treated him like something other than an outcast. Only Sorrik had expressed concern for Ned rather than disdain, contempt, or rejection. Right after the concert, Sorrik had done everything possible to offer reassurance, solace, and help. He had (despite his age) assisted Ned afterward in his frantic effort to capture the loose birds and cart away the toppled cages. He had even spoken with Ned later, up in his workshop—had spoken with him throughout the afternoon and into the evening—as they struggled to make sense of the day's events.

"I'm a failure!" Ned had blurted out to the old man.

"Nonsense," Sorrik had responded, speaking calmly.

"A total, absolute failure."

"Oh, stop this nonsense! Self-pity serves no purpose—you'll just waste your time. And mine as well."

Ned looked up at his friend. Seated in one of just two chairs in the workshop, Sorrik looked stern but not angry. With his wrinkle-soft face and his wispy beard, he resembled a benevolent billy goat. Ned asked him, "How was the avian calliope anything but a failure?"

"Ah, that's an altogether different question," said Sorrik. "Yes indeed, the calliope failed. But you said a moment earlier that *you* were the failure—which is decidedly not the case."

Shaking his head in dismay, Ned went on: "I'm the First Order Apprentice to the Lord High Builder of Instruments. My role within Sifirithi and within the Realm is to build instruments. That and only that. Every moment of every day I work to create new instruments whose music will move the mind and touch the heart. Isn't that why the Masters granted me this role? Isn't the fulfillment of that duty what they expect from me? My purpose in life is to make instruments. Sorrik, I *am* my instruments! If my instruments fail, I fail."

The old man smiled.

"Do you understand what I'm saying?"

Another smile. "Perhaps."

"Perhaps what?" Ned started to feel exasperated with his friend.

"Perhaps I understand that you're a bright, earnest young man," Sorri told him, "one who is just starting to explore the world. I understand, too, that you're blaming yourself for a regrettable sequence of events. Events that added up and made one another worse and worse, much as a stone rolls down hill and knocks loose two more, which then dislodge several more, which then knock loosen still more and more, then more and more and more, until half the mountainside is sliding down and crushing everyone in its path. Who could have predicted that a sparrow would arrive just then? Would arrive at the least likely and worst possible moment! Who could have known that the little bird's song would prompt such a wild response from the others? Such commotion. Such—panic. Who could have imagined that the entire calliope—the whole huge, beautiful instrument you had created—would then collapse under the strain of the captive birds' desperation to escape?"

"It did collapse," Ned told him. "And it was my fault."

"Let me finish. Finally, I understand that you attribute this unfortunate incident to massive flaws in your own character."

Ned wasn't going to refute this claim. It was exactly how Ned felt about the situation, but he knew better than to argue further with his friend. Discouraged, he said only, "I've tried so hard."

"I know that very well."

"I've invented some of the most unusual instruments ever made."

"You have indeed."

"Some of the most elaborate and complex."

"That too," said Sorrik. Then, after a moment's hesitation, the old man went on: "Perhaps we need instruments that aren't more elaborate and complex. Perhaps we need ones that are simpler instead."

"Simpler?"

The old man now reached out and placed his hands on Ned's shoulders. Was this gesture an embrace—or an effort to hold him at arm's length? Ned couldn't be sure. "Listen to me," Sorrik told him. "I would be willing—no, delighted—to speak with you further. To continue discussing these matters. But it's already late, I'm an old man, and I can no longer stay up talking all night long—at least not unless I sleep for two days afterward!"

"Forgive me."

"Don't apologize. This is my limitation, not yours. More to the point, I have to leave early tomorrow morning."

"Another trip to the Lowland?"

"Exactly. To investigate yet another rumor of yet another young person with a remarkable voice. Well, there's no way to know but go there, meet her, and listen."

Sorrik had left Ned's workshop a short while later. In the four days since then, Ned had heard nobody mention anything about him— neither regarding Sorrik's departure from Sifirithi nor his likely return. Ned had missed him. Such an odd fellow, lean as a hungry cat. So cordial, though, and so accepting of Ned's difficulties. He could only look forward with eagerness to the old man's return.

Which, hearing shouts from below, Ned realized might now be imminent. He walked over to the window.

Guards, opening the huge gates, had allowed a coach to enter Sifirithi. Peering out the window, Ned saw the carriers stride into the city with the coach on their shoulders, then work their way through several twists and turns of the cobbled streets, and, after disappearing once or twice into some of the fissure-like alleyways, proceed all the way to the Ministry of Newcomers. The coach soon grew more difficult to see clearly. When the carriers stopped and set down their burden, however, and when its two passengers emerged from inside, Ned could identify Sorrik not just by his black Emissary robes but by his mane of white hair. Sorrik indeed.

With him was—? Ned couldn't tell. Someone female, it seemed, but he couldn't see her well. Distinguishing a woman from a man could be difficult among Lowlanders, at least at a distance, given their shapeless, dirty clothes. Gray-brown homespun garb. Not robes, ex-actly—more like rough cloth bags of the kinds that farmers fill with wheat or potatoes, only with holes cut for the arms and head. Oh well, Ned thought; it hardly mattered. Just another ignorant child to join the choirs.

At least Sorrik had returned: Sorrik the hunter with his latest quar-ry.

III

THE NEWCOMER

6

I n this way Allu reached her destination. The coach arrived at a massive gate—tall as a house—and the carriers halted. At once several guards peered into the coach through the windows, stared at Allu, and conversed with Sorrik. Allu couldn't follow their exchange. Something about a manifest . . . Allu felt too frightened by the sight of these huge men in dark robes to ask any questions. The old emissary handed over some papers, the guards looked at them, and further discussion ensued. The only word that Allu understood was Newcomer. She expected these men to order her out of the coach and then punish her in whatever way Newcomers suffered on arrival in Sifirithi. By now she had began trembling. She tried to stop but couldn't. More than just frightened, she felt deeply sad as she grasped her likely fate. Nothing good could happen in Sifirithi. Then at last the guards backed away, the carriers lifted the coach again, the gate stuttered open, and the coach passed through.

Allu glanced at Sorrik as if to ask what would become of her.

His only answer was a smile.

Would such a kind man allow anyone to harm her? Or was his kindness merely sugar coating a bitter pill that she would soon have to swallow?

She distracted herself by looking out the window. Never in her life had Allu seen such a vast town. More than a town: an entire city. Constructed of dark gray stone, its houses rose taller than any in Laro, rising several stories, sometimes higher; and when the coach crossed an intersection, where Allu could gaze two or three blocks up the streets, she saw numerous, much larger buildings nestled together on slopes that tilted steeper and steeper until they became the great mountainsides looming over Sifirithi. Few people were out at such an early hour, so she couldn't see many of the inhabitants. Even so, she understood at once that this city contained more people than she had met in all of her life up to that moment.

The coach stopped. After a brief silence, voices reached her: first the head carrier announcing her arrival, then people calling back to him. At once someone opened the door. A wide, black-haired woman in a red-and-gray robe stood there. "Welcome," she stated firmly.

"I thank you," Sorrik replied. He stretched, eased out of his seat, and cautiously stepped down from the coach.

"I trust the journey has not been too strenuous?" asked the woman.

"Strenuous enough," the old man said, "but at least it's over."

"The Newcomer—is she well?"

"You should ask her yourself."

"Poor child," said the woman, reaching out to Allu and helping her from the cramped coach. "Such a hardship, traveling up from the Lowland. Well, soon enough we'll soothe you with food, new clothes, and a warm place to sleep."

Allu couldn't help but feel calmed and reassured by these words and by this woman's gentle tone. Or perhaps these words, too, were only sweetness coating foul medicine. What harshness would she soon taste?

"Come with me," said the woman.

Too tired and cold to resist, Allu followed her away from the coach. From there they proceeded through a stone archway, through a doorway, down a hallway, up a staircase, through more hallways, and past men and women who stared at Allu as she passed. Sorrik accompanied them. "Where are you taking me?" Allu asked suddenly.

The woman's only answer: "To where you can sing."

Where you can sing. For a village girl just arrived from the Lowland, these words were like saying *Where you can condemn yourself* or *Where you can doom yourself.*

Allu couldn't resist: her fatigue made her weak. She felt reassured to some degree that Sorrik still walked beside her. Yet why, she asked herself, should she trust him? It's true that he had brought her to Sifirithi himself, and he had done nothing to harm Allu in any way. But of course if a trapper had caught a rabbit in the forest and now brought her to the marketplace, then that trapper, like Sorrik, would have done nothing to harm the creature that he now prepared to relinquish. Her grim fate would come later.

She couldn't think clearly about anything she saw or heard. Couldn't think about the men and women who lingered nearby, each of them attired in long robes—some of intricately patterned wool, some of fur, some of strange materials that Allu couldn't even recognize—men and women who gazed at her from intersecting corridors as she passed. Couldn't think about the vast size of this torch-lit building as she strode into its depths. Or about the sounds she heard in these corridors, sounds that must have been voices . . . voices singing. She couldn't think, couldn't let herself feel. All she wanted was a hearth, some hot food, and a fur robe like what many of the people around her wore. But there was no hearth, food, or robe for Allu yet: only hallways and staircases, one after another, each somehow bigger than the previous, until at last she and her attendants reached a door at the end of a long hallway. After a moment's hesitation, Sorrik opened that door and motioned for Allu to follow him.

They entered a hall so vast that Allu's own house in Laro could have fit within it—and not just the house, but even the oak trees surrounding it. She held back a moment, amazed and afraid. Then a hearth distracted her, a hearth in which flaming logs snapped and popped, calling to Allu with a promise of warmth and wellbeing. Allu restrained the impulse to move closer and warm herself. She was intent on behaving better than a mere villager. She followed Sorrik instead.

More people awaited her. Two men and two women sat on the other side of a huge black table. All four of them wore robes whose fur made them look bigger than they could have been, like woodland beasts; yet she saw something delicate about these three people, too: their lean, pale hands and faces. Allu saw how closely they watched her. Shivering before them in the cold, she felt as vulnerable as if standing there naked.

The tallest and palest of the men said, "The girl from Laro?"

"Yes, Master," replied Sorrik.

This pale man looked Allu up and down. His red, watery eyes made her uneasy. What caught her attention most of all, however, was the robe he wore, its surface stitched over with little brittle sticks that clicked and ticked as he shifted.

Sorrik told Allu, "This is the Master of Newcomers. He wishes to ask you a few questions."

Allu hesitated to draw near—she wanted only to step closer to the hearth.

The Master asked, "What is your name?"

"Allu," she answered, her voice almost too faint to hear.

"Allu. Yes, Allu. We have heard much of you. Tell me, how old are you?"

She tried speaking, but nothing happened. Then she whispered, "Sixteen."

Sorrik said, "She is tired and hungry. The journey has weakened her."

"No doubt," said the Master, "but we need the girl to give us a notion of her gift." Glancing a moment at the emissary, he then turned to Allu. "Tell me this: do you like to sing?"

Allu nodded yes, then shook her head no. She kept recalling all the warnings she had heard; warnings from as far back as she could remember; warnings about the dangers of singing. *Don't sing, Allu, or the Masters will take you away to Sifirithi.*

The old man stood, pushed back his chair, and, clicking intricately, walked carefully around the table. He reached out to Allu. She nearly pulled away but restrained herself: he looked harmless enough, almost frail, in his enormous robe. He said, "Come by the fire, my child—yes, come with me. We will find warm clothing and food for you soon. Please forgive our impatience."

His reassurance wasn't what calmed Allu; it was the promise of warmth. She stepped closer to the hearth, reached out to the flames, and wiggled her fingers as if shaking off the chill that had soaked into her bones. Then, abruptly, she remembered not to behave like a village girl. She stopped. She looked around. No one spoke. She caught sight of the two women and the man still sitting behind the table and watching her. Had she done something foolish? Something wrong?

Sorrik said, "She will sing for us now."

Uneasy, Allu said, "I can't."

"What?" asked the old man, his face showing dismay. "Why not?"

"I just—can't."

"One little tune. A few notes. Anything."

Allu felt too cold to respond.

"She can barely talk," said the Master of Newcomers, which reassured Allu until he added, "Which promises little for singing."

Sorrik said, "Her voice is flawless—as pure as water."

"Right now it seems less substantial than steam."

Allu looked at them helplessly. All she could do was keep warming herself.

Sorrik turned to her again and said, "Please, Allu—sing for us." Then to the Master: "She is everything I have claimed her to be."

Allu looked at these people and wondered what they wanted. If she sang, would they reward her—or punish her? She couldn't decide what to do. All of them stared at her. Even Sorrik stared. She realized at that moment how difficult even a simple task had become: it was one task to sing, quite another to sing with everyone listening. Allu looked down at the floor.

After a moment of silence, Sorrik told her, "You heard the Master. You must sing."

She said nothing.

"Sing for the Master."

Still no answer.

"Allu, this is what you have come here to do. What you have wanted to do. What are you waiting for?" He gestured awkwardly to the others: "Forgive her—she is easily upset."

"I won't sing till the music comes," Allu said abruptly.

Puzzled, no one responded at first. Then someone asked, "Music? Shall we bring her some pages to read from?"

At once Allu said, "No, I mean the music inside. Inside *me*."

A mutter of puzzlement and dismay arose. Allu watched these people, listened to them, and wondered yet again what would become of her. She might end up back in Laro sooner than she had imagined. Or would she never see home again? A thought of her family flitted through her mind—her parents' uneasy discussion of the plan to send her away, her family's awkward farewell—and she pushed their voices back. There would be plenty of time to hear them. Why couldn't the other voices come to her now?

"—and give her one last chance, Master," Sorrik was saying. "She deserves it. You deserve it. For no matter how meek she seems—"

"Enough," the Master told him.

"Surely—"

"I said *enough*. We have given her a chance. You have had chances, too, Sorrik. How many more peasants will you bring us? How much longer shall we wait while you coax a few notes from their rough little tongues? Haven't we given you enough chances already?"

Listening, Allu grew frightened. Sorrik looked helpless standing before the Masters. She wanted to rush forth and stop this attack on the person who had been so kind to her.

The song came to her at once. Allu winced as if someone had struck her. Gasping, the first note was more of a cry than a note; then she caught her breath, steadied herself, and sang. Allu sang easily, lightly, gently as rain. She sang without effort. She sang and sang, as startled as everyone else, since even Allu herself hadn't heard the song before.

> My dreams are flowers that bloomed all night.
> Now, cut and dried, they're pressed within the book of sleep.
> But when I go to bed this evening, light
> Will fade and dreams will bloom again to pluck and keep.

Somehow her song warmed Allu as much as the fire did, only better: warmed her from the inside out. She sang a while longer, then stopped.

No one spoke. No one moved. Everyone in the room—the Master of Newcomers, other Masters, Sorrik, even Allu herself—just stood there. After a few moments, this lack of sound and lack of motion started to frighten Allu almost as much as the harsh words preceding her song. Surely these people felt angry at her.

Then she knew better. Something had changed. She saw it even in the Master of Newcomers, who looked at her now with a softer light in his eyes.

He said, "Yes, I understand."

7

D anger had turned to safety, defeat to victory. The Masters nodded to one another, smiling, and welcomed Allu to Sifirithi. The Master of Newcomers even clasped her hands. "Show her to the Low Hall," he told Sorrik, "and make sure that the cooks feed her well. The poor girl is almost too weak to sing." He waved everyone away with an impatient gesture.

Allu left eagerly. This turn of events amazed her. She felt no fear now, only relief. What, exactly, had she done? Somehow she had pleased these people, though Allu herself wasn't sure how.

Nothing of what Sorrik did next disappointed her. Striding through a sequence of corridors, he led Allu to her room in a stone tower overlooking a courtyard. Even before she could try the bed—which, covered with vast fur blankets, looked impossibly huge and warm—two maids-in-waiting entered, each carrying an armful of garments. At once they started offering Allu a choice of attire.

"For me?" asked Allu, baffled.

"Of course," Sorrik responded. "You must dress properly for the Low Choir."

Allu put on a gray woolen robe without speaking. What could she have said? The robe's smoothness and warmth left her mute. Then, before she could examine any of the other clothes, a servant arrived with a tray and began setting out plates and bowls of food on a table near the window. Cakes of some sort. A sweet-smelling porridge. A tiny roasted bird, crouched in gravy. A bowl of berries. A pitcher of steaming milk.

"This is all for *me?*"

The emissary gestured for Allu to sit. "Of course. You must regain your strength."

Ignoring everyone, she seated herself at once, stared at the array of foods on the table, and, snatching up a spoon, abruptly started gobbling the porridge. She had never been so hungry nor had ever felt so delighted with the food she ate.

Sorrik dismissed the servants. As they left he told Allu, "You will be happy here, I'm sure of it. You will be safe and warm. The Low Master will arrange to bring you whatever you want. Best of all, you will sing whenever you like, and no one will stop you."

"No one?"

"No one at all. In fact, many people will sing *with* you."

"But what if they—" Allu fell silent.

"What if they what?"

She looked away, ashamed of herself. "What if they punish me?"

Sorrik only smiled. "They will do nothing of the kind. On the contrary, they will help you. You will help them, too, as you all work together in the Low Choir."

"You will teach us."

Sorrik laughed at her. "Far from it! Teaching singers isn't my honor. Finding them is honor enough."

"You won't be here, then?" Allu asked, suddenly afraid. How would she face all these new experiences without him?

"Don't worry. Other singers will be with you there. The Masters will take good care of you." As the emissary watched Allu, his face grew serious. "I have to go search now for more singers," he said. "That's my honor. But listen: I promise to visit you."

"You must!" Allu exclaimed. She reached over to embrace him.

Sorrik held her warmly and said, "Someone will guide you for a while. She is a young woman like yourself. I brought her from the town of Elasea almost a year ago. She will be kind to you." The emissary turned to leave.

As he crossed the room, Allu called out, "Sorrik—"

"I promise to visit you."

She cheered up quickly. Three servants brought more food. They pulled back the covers from a huge bed and helped Allu into it.

Exhausted, she dozed off even as the servants were stepping out and closing the door.

Sifirithi . . .

At once she roused and sat upright. *Sifirithi.* Had she actually arrived here—arrived in the very place that everyone in the Lowland dreaded, hated, and spoke about only in hushed voices? Was it possible that after hearing so many fearsome words about this distant city, Allu now found herself so warmly received and so well treated?

She flung back the fur blankets, got up, crossed the room, and stepped over to the window.

Sifirithi! The placed looked different from what she had expected. It was big, bigger than any town that Allu had seen, with many stone houses built neatly against one another on the ridge, others set into cliffs on each side, and still others cut out of the mountains that towered above the city. It looked like part of the land yet separate from it, too, as if welling up out of the rock itself. From her room, which looked out over the central area, Allu could see all sorts of streets and alleyways, corridors and passages, bridges and staircases, linking each part of the city to the rest: the high places to the low, the far to the near. A villager like Allu, long accustomed to Laro, found this city huge and complex, a puzzle of many pieces.

She had heard stories about Sifirithi for as long as she could remember. Some were angry stories, some envious; some fearful, some uncertain; some peevish, hostile, or sad. What they told her was simple enough: Allu didn't belong in Sifirithi. The Masters of Sifirithi controlled Laro and all the other villages in Siir; and everyone throughout the land hated all the Masters. The very name Sifirithi could chill any villager's bones.

For a moment, Allu wished she were back home again. Then she thought of her mother, her father, her sisters and her brother . . . How could they have betrayed her so? Didn't they care what happened to her? Or was Allu's departure simply what needed to happen, since the Masters would have punished the whole family otherwise? It puzzled her, too, that no harm had befallen her yet. No one had punished her. In fact, the Master of Newcomers had treated her well.

Allu didn't know what to think.

Unable to answer the questions swarming through her mind like bees, she decided not to struggle. She let them buzz in hopes of their settling down or going away. Soon she felt too tried to think about anything at all. Allu walked over to the bed, lay down, and, without even covering herself with the fur blankets, she fell asleep.

8

She awoke with a start.

Sunbeams now angled into her room through the windows. Allu forced herself up from the bed, stretched, and walked over to take in the view. Although the sky looked lumpy with clouds, enough light shoved past the overcast to illuminate the city. Sifirithi looked even bigger and more complex than the day before. The day before . . . Allu realized that yesterday's events hadn't been a dream: to her lingering astonishment, she was in Sifirithi.

Just then someone knocked on the door. Even before Allu could speak, the door opened, a servant walked in, and this elderly man, neatly dressed in a red-and-gray robe and carrying a tray, served Allu breakfast. She realized at once that her belly ached with hunger.

"For you, my child."

"All of this?" she asked, looking over the plates of pastries and fruits.

"Any and all that might please you."

Allu seated herself at once and began to eat.

"I must tell you, however," said the servant, "that in a short while your guide will arrive here."

"What guide?"

"Your guide to the Low Choir."

This guide turned out to be a young woman named Dessina. She was somewhat older than Allu, perhaps seventeen or eighteen. Her pale skin and uncallused hands suggested a life spent far away from the villages. Dessina wore her long black hair braided, as Allu herself did, but in two ropes of hair rather than just one. Her accent was light, almost airy, and she spoke without contempt or anger. Allu liked her at once—all the more so when Dessina lost no time in showing Allu around and telling her what she needed to know.

As they walked down a long corridor, Allu said, "I never thought I would ever see such a place."

"Well, here you are," replied Dessina. "It's a good thing, too."

With a little coaxing, Allu accompanied Dessina through the Low Hall past kitchens, dining rooms, and courtyards. The place was enormous. Allu would have found it frightening without Dessina; in her companion's presence, however, the Low Hall merely baffled her. "What is it all for?"

"For?" asked Dessina.

"For what purpose."

Dessina smiled. "For us. For the Low Choir. We live here, sleep here, eat here, and study here."

"I know, but I'm still surprised—"

"What other purpose could it serve?"

Shrugging, Allu said, "I don't know. It just seems so—wonderful. All of this just for some people who sing."

Dessina laughed at her. "Don't you like it?"

"Of course I like it—I said it's wonderful. I've never been so happy."

"You have good reason to be happy. All of us do."

They walked for a while without speaking. Dessina led Allu down a flight of stairs, through a huge doorway, and out onto a balcony with a view of the whole city. The low parts of Sifirithi spread out below; the rest rose off to the right and the left. Allu and her new friend walked over to the railing. Wind whipped at them near the edge. Although chilly at first, Allu discovered that she could stay warm by tucking her hands into the sleeves of her new robe.

Allu said, "Such fine garments. Much warmer than my clothes back home."

"There will be better," Dessina told her without looking over.

Surprised, Allu said nothing at first, then asked, "What could be better than this?"

"Bell cloth, for one."

"Bell cloth? What's bell cloth?"

"You'll find out some day—if you prove yourself to the Masters, of course. If not, you'll never need to know."

Allu decided not to ask Dessina for an explanation; she would content herself with standing there and looking out from the balcony. Besides, something surprised her. She didn't see any carts or animals below, just people, so that Sifirithi, despite its size, was much quieter than a village. The lack of noise bothered Allu at first, then pleased her—so different from a crowded place like Laro. Yet she soon discovered that Sifirithi was far from silent. Strange music drifted everywhere. Shapeless and soft, it hung in midair, shifting this way and that, sometimes distant, sometimes nearby, like a pall of fog. Allu stopped, looked about, trying to find its source. She couldn't. It seemed to be everywhere. Music swirled around her.

Then Allu saw Dessina laughing. "What is it?" Allu asked. "Tell me!"

Dessina just kept laughing.

Annoyed now, Allu said, "You have to tell me!"

"Chimes," answered Dessina. "The chimes of Sifirithi." She pointed toward one of the houses below.

Allu saw almost at once that something resembling pieces of heavy wire hung from the eaves. These wires trembled when a breeze came through. Others hung from balconies, still others from the gables above. All at once Allu could see them everywhere: on windows, in doorways, under overhangs. Some looked big: stout as rope. Others looked small: thinner than string. Most of them looked like the string-beans that Allu's mother hung up to dry each autumn. Instead of clattering and rustling like that stark harvest, however, these chimes now rang so gently that a rumbly hum came out of them. Allu listened a moment. Then she asked, "But what are they for?"

Dessina didn't seem to understand.

Allu couldn't repeat her own question. She didn't even try. So many notes poured out, swirled together, and rushed off that the whole city was adrift in music. Allu, caught by surprise, found herself suddenly afloat, happy and unafraid, as the wind passed through Sifirithi and left in its wake something much like the lace a wave spreads out on the sea when it passes.

"You'll have time enough to marvel at Sifirithi," Dessina said. "Right now we must proceed."

"Proceed?" Allu asked. "Proceed where?"

"Where do you think?" was the only answer.

Dessina led her off the balcony, through a series of hallways, up and down a sequence of stairways, and across a stone square. Soon Allu found herself in a large hall. "The Low Choir," Dessina told her.

They had joined dozens of other students in a hall for exercises, practice, and lessons. Most were still half-asleep at that hour—the sun hadn't yet risen over the mountains across the valley—but Allu, at least, didn't protest. Having grown up in a village where every daughter and every son performed daily chores, she was accustomed to such early rising. Besides, her own excitement had woken her at an early hour anyway. The Low Choir! She would gladly have gone without sleep altogether just to sing in the Choir.

Better yet, she found herself among other young people who seemed more like Allu than her own folk in Laro. Their clothing was much different from village attire—gray robes made of soft, beautifully woven wool—but otherwise they looked like ordinary children and teens. They were playfully singing even before the lessons began. Allu started to feel more comfortable among them. At least a hundred members of the Low Choir swarmed out of their eating halls and through the corridors. Some of the older ones went off with their own teachers; some of the younger ones left, too; and those of about Allu's age met in a great hall whose windows looked out to the east and let sunlight enter and fall in great patches across the floor.

"You must come now," Dessina told Allu. "We'll be late if you don't hurry."

Inside, young choristers strayed about, chatting and laughing as they struggled to shake off the night's darkness and chill.

They sang all morning. Sometimes they sang alone, just practicing; they often sang in clusters of five or six; and sometimes they sang together, a hundred singers at once, with everyone standing on benches that rose like a staircase against the wall. Allu felt almost dizzy at first: so many people, so much activity, so much noise! Even a harvest-time marketplace in Laro would have been calm by comparison. Yet she felt happy to be there, and she took to her studies like a hungry girl sitting down to a feast.

Allu practiced for a while with some other singers, including Dessina, who taught her warm-up scales and a few other exercises, who laughed agreeably when she tried imitating them, and who then led her to the benches where everyone else had begun gathering.

"This will be the day's lesson," Dessina told Allu. "Come now: here is the Low Master."

Before Allu could ask any questions, her companion took her by the hand, led her up a few steps, and showed her where to stand on the benches. Other people took their own places as well. Many dozens of singers, all of them wearing gray woolen robes, stood in long rows. There was some good-natured teasing and shoving for a while; then everyone settled into silence. Looking past her companions' shoulders and heads, Allu could see a small man dressed in strange clothes standing before the Choir. He appeared to be speaking.

Allu asked Dessina, "Who is he?"

"The Low Master, just as I told you. Now hush."

Allu stifled her other questions.

"—for the wellbeing of all in Siir," the Low Master was saying. "We must therefore live up to the honor granted us. We must excel at our task. It is for our own good. It is for the good of Sifirithi. It is, above all, for the good of the Harmonor."

"What's he talking about?"

"I told you, hush!"

The Master spoke for a long time. Allu listened, more uncertain now than before, and kept watching. This man didn't make sense. Live up to the honor? For the good of Sifirithi? Yet he looked calm and content, as if he knew exactly what he wanted. Allu kept listening. She stared at the man. Like everyone else here, he was small and pale. His clothing caught her attention. He wore garments that appeared to be fur, but which, as Allu looked closer, turned out to be something else altogether. Little sticks covered the man's body, bristly as a porcupine's quills, but so abundant that they looked like cloth; and as he moved, those sticks rustled like autumn insects in a field. Listening, Allu felt so puzzled that all she wanted was to start singing.

The master soon gave her a chance. He said, "Now we shall return to what we started yesterday: Exercise Four Hundred Sixty-six."

A pause followed. Allu didn't notice when the silence ended and the singing began. The music rose from the choir as gently as mist from a lake. The Master nodded and gestured, drawing it forth. Gradually, the sound grew louder, first on one side, then on the other, then both at once. Allu glanced about, listened, and wondered what to do. There was no melody, just the rise and fall of those voices; and although this exercise seemed simple, far simpler than the melodies that had come to her in Laro, she couldn't follow it well enough to respond. She just stood there. When the Master looked in her direction at one point, Allu opened her mouth and swayed like some of the others; but as soon as the Master looked elsewhere, she stopped. The music had grown louder already. Allu listened. It was strange. She managed to join in a little—a few notes at first, then more, then almost all of them—but without much interest.

Somehow Allu had expected to sing real music: tunes and songs, at least, or perhaps ballads like what foreigners sang when they foolishly strayed into Siir; or perhaps something else altogether, strange and mysterious, since this was, after all, Sifirithi. This exercise disappointed her. Pleasant enough, neither too loud nor too soft. Simple. Allu joined the others again, discovering that she could sing these notes without effort. It was easy. Sometimes her dreamsongs left her exhausted, as if she hadn't sung them, but had been sung by them. By contrast, Exercise Four Hundred Sixty-six was much gentler. Yet she kept waiting for something to . . . *happen*. Anything! It never did. The Choir sang and sang. The notes came forth. A pall of music hung over the Choir like spring fog. Allu struggled to stay awake.

What surprised her more than the music itself was why anyone bothered singing at all. Yet other singers took part in this exercise as if not only willing but eager. Allu watched them. At first she wondered if she might be mistaken. This shapeless music wasn't so bad, was it? Gentle, relaxing, calm . . . Surely a little more effort would make it worthwhile. Then Allu realized that she couldn't continue. She couldn't even start again. Exercise Four Hundred Sixty-six felt so pointless that her voice withered inside her. She scarcely managed to stay patient until the lesson ended.

"Isn't it wonderful?" asked Dessina afterward. "The Choir! The Exercises! I'm sure being here is even better than you expected."

Allu nodded. "I suppose so it is."

"The Low Master teaches us so much—teaches us exactly what we need to know."

"He does. He certainly does." She faltered, falling silent. Then she asked, "But what is it? I mean, what does he teach us?"

Dessina laughed at Allu. "Why, the Exercises."

Unable to restrain herself, Allu blurted out: "What are they? They didn't seem like anything at all. You call that music? Even the humming of bees would make a better tune!"

"I don't know what you're talking about," Dessina said, looking more surprised than angry. "I don't understand what you're saying."

Allu stopped short. "The music— What we sang— It seemed too—simple."

"It *is* simple."

"Is that—all? Don't we get to sing anything better?"

Dessina looked more and more uneasy. "You shouldn't ask what else we'll sing," she told Allu. "This is only the Low Choir."

"I'm only asking—"

"Even the biggest castle needs a foundation—something to support the structure above. Work hard, learn carefully, and perhaps someday you'll ascend to the Middle Choir."

"The Middle Choir?"

"If you ascend, you'll learn about it soon enough. If you don't, then you won't need to know, will you?"

Cheering up, Allu said, "Well, then: I want to ascend—and soon!"

"When the time is right," Dessina told her. Then she added, "Don't worry about ascending. The Middle Master will call you if you're honored. Right now, you can best serve Sifirithi in the Low Choir."

Though puzzled and displeased, Allu went along with Dessina's suggestion. She studied her lessons over the next few days. She sang in the Low Choir. She joined in the musical games that her companions played during their free time. She said nothing further about how much she disliked the exercises and everything else that the Low Master taught his young students. This was all for the best, Allu told herself. It wasn't so bad. Better than milking goats and hauling firewood in Laro, certainly. Maybe Dessina was right. Work hard, learn well. It was an honor to be in Sifirithi.

She grew comfortable as the days passed. Allu always had enough to eat. She always felt warm enough. Servants did whatever she asked of them: made her bed, brought her clean robes, closed the shutters when the sun went down. Best of all, Allu had a friend for the first time in her life. Perhaps more than one, since surely all the singers, more than a hundred of them, were Allu's friends. She couldn't tell them everything that passed through her mind, but they were friends anyway. They taught her, joked with her, and laughed when she teased them. And no one made Allu stop singing.

9

Something else pleased Allu: the voices kept coming to her. Sometimes while dreaming and sometimes while awake, she heard songs that came and went, quick as migrating birds; she heard songs that lingered a while, then faded; she even heard songs that struck without warning, swept her about, and left her exhausted and frightened when they departed. Allu didn't know what to make of these songs when they welled up inside her. At times she wearied of them. If they stayed away, however, as they sometimes did for a few days, she felt restless and unhappy. Allu called out to these voices: first gently, then firmly, soon desperately. She hoped they would return. She feared they wouldn't. She waited and waited.

They came in their own time; they came in their own way.

Once, while at Choir, Allu heard the voices. They sang so lovely a tune that she couldn't help but sing with them even though she happened to be in the Low Choir just then and was singing its music. Allu tried to resist. The voices caught her up. She felt no way to ignore those voices. Their song was water in the desert.

Just then she noticed the Master watching her. Everyone in the Low Choir had fallen silent. Only the Master's robe made any sound: a rustling noise like wind in a wheatfield. The Master said, "You in the third row: yes, you. What is the matter?"

Allu couldn't answer him.

"Are you not feeling well?"

The Master's concern reassured Allu. She whispered, "Yes. No. I mean, no."

"What is the matter, then? Are you singing or not?"

Allu fell silent again.

The Master stepped closer and stood right before the front-row singers. Although Allu felt safe behind them for a moment, some of the choristers stepped aside to reveal her. She felt uneasy in the Master's gaze. His face bothered Allu: angular as the mountains outside. Yet he didn't look angry but concerned. "You must be ill, my child."

"No," Allu told him. "I'm well."

"You are not singing."

"I am singing."

"I saw you stop."

"Yes, I stopped."

"Then why have you told me you were singing?"

"Because sometimes I sing and sometimes I stop."

A few of the other singers began whispering to one another.

The Master said, "Children, be still." Then to Allu: "Why did you stop? Who asked you to stop?"

"No one, but—"

"Then why did you stop?"

Allu hesitated again. Then, almost against her will, she started singing.

> Rose, heather, daisy, thistle—
> Each is a flower that blooms so long.

"Where did you learn that song?" the Master asked, his expression showing surprise.

> Joint, muscle, tendon, gristle—
> Each is a flesh that makes us strong.

The Master now gazed at her in dismay. "I said, Where did you learn that song?"

"Nowhere."

The Master stepped closer. The Low Choir parted to make way for him. He stood right before Allu. Allu had never been so near to this man. His appearance startled her. His strange garment looked like a soldier's chain-mail, only made of sticks instead of metal. "No one sings such a song without learning it," he said, "least of all a girl like you."

Allu didn't know what to say. "It is an old song—a village song, Master."

"Village song? Where are you from?"

"Laro, Master."

"All songs are prohibited in the Lowland."

"It is an old song."

"This is strange talk," the Master told Allu, "and a strange song." He stared at his student for a while. "Would you sing it for me again?"

Although reluctant, she said, "Maybe."

"Maybe?"

She braced herself for the blow. Nothing happened. The Master just stood there, watching and waiting even more intently than before. The other students watched silently around him.

Allu couldn't think what to do. She felt captive there, and nothing chased the voices off faster than a sense of captivity. The more she wanted to sing, the less she could feel the music present inside her.

"Where is the song?" asked the Master.

She stared at her feet. Sunlight lay upon the floor in great panels. The room was so silent she could almost hear the light slipping across the tiles.

"Shall I wait here all day?"

Allu wanted to answer, she tried answering, but she couldn't speak even a single word. She looked up at the Master, then away.

He said, "All song has fled you, it seems. Just as I suspected—"

More and more frightened now, Allu tried to leave—she would walk off, would leave the Low Choir, would run away from Sifirithi— but she found herself helpless. All she could do was stand there.

"I have tried to be patient," the Master explained. "I have tried to be gentle. We do not often have students from the Lowland. For good reason: you are all rough and lazy. You are full of high spirits but empty of discipline. Small wonder that the Masters of Sifirithi rarely tolerate—"

Allu stopped listening to the Master when the other voices returned.

> Eyes, ears, nose, fingers—
> These are the parts that give us senses—

She could hear the Low Master, but only at a distance, much as Allu, when crossing a meadow back in Laro, might have continued to hear a cow's mooing even as a lark's song caught her attention. What she heard was the music that the Master had interrupted. And she knew even before she herself joined in the singing that those inner voices had saved her.

IV

CROSSING PATHS

10

One course of action might help, Ned decided: to find Sorrik
once again and speak with him further. The old man would offer insights on how to proceed. How should Ned resume work
following his recent humiliation in the Great Circle? How could he
make sense of the Lord High Builder's comment?—*You must redeem
yourself.* How could he prepare for whatever the Lord High Builder
and the other Masters now expected of him? How might he meet
their expectations and regain their approval? How, in short, could
he salvage his honor? With Sorrik now back from the Lowland, Ned
would locate him and seek his counsel.

Ned therefore left his workshop, descended the staircases leading
from his mountainside down to the Great Circle, and strode through
the city to the cluster of low buildings that housed the various Em-
issaries. Arriving at Sorrik's quarters, he knocked on the door and
waited. No response. Sorrik had never minded if Ned, dropping by
unannounced, entered his room, so he did just that. "All in harmony?" he called out. No answer. The room looked as it always did:
almost empty. If Ned hadn't known the old man better, he would
have thought this room uninhabited. A low, hard bed was the only
furniture. A small wooden box rested near the bed. A woven mat lay
in the middle of the wooden floor. A single window brought light into
the room. Ned had always felt astonished that such a warm, cordial
person could live in such a stark place, but he had learned over the
years not to put much stock in Sorrik's external circumstances. In
his own way, the old man warmed and illuminated his surroundings
no matter where he was at the time. The starkness of this room said
nothing about him. Where was he, though? Perhaps at the Hall of

Newcomers? Having arrived back in Sifirithi just the previous morning, Sorrik would surely have returned there to help that Lowland lass get settled. Yes, the Hall of Newcomers.

Ned set off at once.

He worked his way toward the Great Circle, where he heard snatches of the Middle Choir's anthems as that group practiced. He crossed the Circle's expanse. He entered the marketplace and worked his way among the stalls where vendors sold meat, vegetables, potatoes, grain, fish, and housewares, with all of the men and women calling out with their vendors' songs. He passed some Healers singing to a sick old woman who had apparently collapsed and now rested limply on the cobblestones. He passed a squadron of Song Guards restraining a pickpocket with their shackle-like melody. Then, working his way up the lower slope of the Lesser Mountain, he started the final stretch of his journey.

At every point of this walk, Ned had crossed paths with people he knew, and he greeted each one of them: "All in harmony."

"All in harmony," they sang in return.

No, not harmony, he thought as he passed them. In *dissonance*—like two singers singing notes out of tune with each other. People acknowledged him but didn't fully meet his gaze. Some who ordinarily would have stopped to chat now turned away. A few pretended not to notice him.

All right, then, Ned told them in the silence of his own mind. Treat me like an exile even though I remain here among you.

He felt relieved to reach the Hall of Newcomers.

Yet as he looked around, he saw no sign of Sorrik.

Then he spotted Dessina, Second Order Guardian of Newcomers, and greeted her: "All in harmony."

"All in harmony," she sang. Smiling in amusement, she stated, "What a fine surprise to see you here."

"I'm looking for Sorrik," he replied. Ned couldn't have been more pleased to find Dessina before him now. Her light gray robe provided a perfect background for the young maiden's hair, which was altogether black and long enough to reach almost to the floor. Obsidian eyes, high cheekbones, beautifully sculpted nose, and smooth skin—the sight of her features always stirred his admiration and longing.

She taunted him: "You would visit this hall to make an old man the object of your quest!"

Ned couldn't tell if her taunt expressed amusement or offense. "Indeed I would, since I'm here only on business," he told her. "If I were visiting for pleasure, I would be seeking someone else."

"Reassuring words to hear."

"I in turn feel pleased you find them reassuring."

"Indeed. Though I must admit," she added, "I would find at least as much reassurance in certain words spoken by the Lord High Master of Marriages."

"No doubt the Master will speak when she's ready."

"No doubt."

"Till then, what can one do but wait?"

"What indeed?"

They continued in this manner for a while, circling each other as cats do when it's uncertain if they intend to nuzzle each other—or lash out with exposed claws.

At last Dessina said, "Regarding Sorrik—I haven't seen him since early this morning, but he stopped by earlier to visit the girl he just brought up from the Lowland."

"I saw him arrive with her a few days ago."

"He's attentive anyway, but more so than usual with this new one."

"Why is that?" Ned asked.

"Who knows!" Dessina exclaimed. "Let's just say it's good that she sounds better than she looks. She's as wild as a weasel. I can't remember a time when we've received such a rude, uncivilized girl in our midst. Even for a Lowlander she's nothing but trouble."

"Surely she wasn't chosen for her behavior."

"True. But everyone finds her stubborn and uncouth."

"No doubt the Masters will teach her some manners—or else will send her back to the Lowland."

Dessina smiled dismissively. "No doubt. As for your ancient friend: the Low Choir Hall is the place to start. I just left there myself, but I'm off now to run an errand for the Master."

"Thank you," Ned replied. "All in harmony."

"All in harmony," she sang, then turned to leave, her black cape of hair swishing back and forth as she walked away.

Ned strode down the stone corridor, reached the Low Choir soon enough, and, carefully opening the massive oak door, entered the choir hall. No doubt the singers would be practicing; he didn't want to disturb them. He would find out soon enough if Sorrik was present. Thus he entered the anteroom and eased the door shut without a sound. Then, letting his eyes adjust to the dimmer light, he stepped into the hall itself.

The Low Choir was indeed in session. Several dozen singers stood at the far side of the hall, each of them attired in drab gray robes. The Low Master faced them, his back to Ned. Rather than directing one of the anthems, however, he was addressing them in a calm but stern voice. Such was the fate of the Low Choristers: they had so much to learn that the Master often scolded them for their ignorance. Still, the Master's tone of voice at that particular moment suggested so much perplexity and astonishment that Ned could only wonder what had prompted it. For this reason, he crossed the back of the hall, walked quietly down a side aisle, and, partially hidden by a dark stone column rising from the floor to the ceiling high above, he drew closer to the singers arrayed in rows at the front of the hall. Did any of them notice his approach? Apparently not, for no one betrayed any awareness of his presence. The Low Master, facing away, certainly didn't catch sight of him.

Ned realized right away that the object of the Master's attention was, in fact, the Newcomer who Sorrik had brought up from the Lowland. At once Ned felt compelled to stare at the incident now unfolding before him. In particular, he stared at the Newcomer.

Such a plain appearance! Her mouth, nose, brow, and beady brown eyes looked ordinary, even crude, revealing the absence of refinement that Ned had observed so often in Lowlanders. Her ruddy, wind-burned face suggested too much time spent outdoors, much of that time surely wasted on rough Lowland tasks such as tilling the soil, cultivating crops, and herding animals. Her hands, too, were red-dish from excessive work. Her disheveled hair, brown as dirt and cut roughly braided, made her look like an ill-bred, half-wild ten-year-old rather than a young woman. Her body was so lean that the robe she wore hung on her as loosely as an old blanket thrown over a scare-crow's shoulders. The effect of these features combined in such a way that this girl, standing now among the members of the Low Choir, resembled a forest hare that had somehow wandered into a hutch full of tame, plump, well-groomed rabbits. Ned couldn't help but find the sight of her amusing and contemptible.

What could the Masters have in mind, allowing this peasant into Sifirithi? Why had they let her join even the Low Choir? What could this country girl have to offer?

Then she sang.

At first Ned didn't know what was happening. His flesh responded before his mind had any chance: his neck tingled, his back shivered, and his face warmed as if on a hot summer day. Almost at once an odd, unfamiliar pleasure welled up within him. If her song had been a flavor to taste rather than a sound to hear, Ned would have felt like a bee hovering before a flower, drinking the nectar cupped there and finding perfect sweetness. He savored it, feeling at once delighted and amazed.

> There's nothing old,
> There's nothing new—
> There's nothing in between.

Ned could see that he wasn't alone in his response. Members of the Low Choir, too, showed signs of astonishment at this Newcomer: how they gazed at her. The Master of the Low Choir, too, simply stared and listened.

No one spoke.

> There's nothing dark,
> There's nothing light—
> There's nothing to be seen.

The girl kept singing. Ned, lost in the maze of her melody, couldn't recall where he was. He lost track of time. Never in his life had he heard a song like this one. The Low Choir generally sang simple, stark exercises, so Ned wouldn't have expected anything lush or complex from this group; even if he had been visiting the Middle or High Choirs, however, Ned would have felt startled and confused to hear anyone sing like this Newcomer. As if he had reached out to touch a piece of crude homespun wool but felt silk instead, he couldn't fully understand the difference between his expectation and his experience.

All he knew was that something dormant within him now roused and wakened.

To his surprise, however, Ned saw the Low Choir's Master showing signs of perplexity, not pleasure. The Newcomer's strange song held the Master's attention, but his brow tightened, his eyes watched intently, and his mouth showed nothing like a smile.

The Newcomer finished singing.

A long silence followed.

Then, speaking calmly but firmly to everyone present, the Master said, "The session is over. You may leave now, all of you."

The Low Choristers looked back at him in puzzlement. Leave now? Early? They had surely never heard such a command before— not from any of the Masters, but least of all from the Master of the Low Choir, a demanding teacher notorious for working his students hard and long, often far longer than the time allotted for their sessions. For this reason they hesitated.

"I do not intend to repeat myself," he told them. Extending his right hand with the palm upward, he gestured toward the door.

The students now descended from the steps and, with the Lowland lass still among them, everyone began to leave.

The Master's voice cut them short: "You—the Newcomer. Stay. Come here."

When she turned, the Newcomer looked stricken. "Me?" she asked.

"You."

Everyone else left as fast as possible, each eager to avoid the taint of whatever poison the Master had detected in the girl's song.

Ned, still unnoticed where he stood half-hidden, paid keen attention. He was dismayed, however, that the Master happened to be facing away from him. Ned could neither follow the man's words nor hear much of the Newcomer's responses, since the Master's body—large in its own right and larger because of the massive robe he wore—blocked her voice.

Gesturing, he seemed to be asking her a question.

Of the girl's reply, Ned caught only one word: "—song—"

The Master asked another question.

"—don't know—"

Then another question.

"—believe so, Master," she answered.

The exchange proceeded in this manner for a while, the Master calmly interrogating the Newcomer, the girl responding briefly and firmly. Ned felt tempted to draw closer. Perhaps the Master's and the Newcomer's mutual attention would allow Ned to approach unnoticed. Then he thought better of intruding. Surely they would spot him. His presence would disrupt their conversation. Better to let them proceed. Better to keep silent, to wait, and to ask Sorrik later on what he knew about the situation.

At some point he realized that the force preventing his departure wasn't mere curiosity. He also felt concern about this Newcomer. First, because the Master beckoned to one of his assistants—a lean, gray-haired woman—who listened to his private comments, then hurried away. That sense of urgency was remarkable in its own right: no one ever made a fuss over a Newcomer. Second, the Master continued to converse with the Lowlander in a way that suggested intense curiosity. He didn't raise his voice, but Ned knew enough about him to know that he wasn't questioning her out of mere amusement. Nobody ever sang unbidden for this Master. Doing so would invariably earn some sort of punishment. No doubt she would deserve it, too—she was, after all, so recently arrived in Sifirithi. Yet Ned couldn't help but feel some kind of protectiveness toward her: the same protectiveness, perhaps, that he might have felt if he'd spotted a cat corner a little bird.

His concern intensified when, just a short while later, the assistant arrived with two other people. One was a man who Ned recognized as the Lord High Master of the Middle Choir. The other was a tall woman dressed in a robe of finely patterned gray, white, orange, and red weave—someone Ned had never seen before. He felt reassured only that the Master of Newcomers hadn't summoned the Song Guards to drag this girl away. But requesting the presence of these Masters: Ned couldn't even guess why they would pay so much attention now to this Lowlander.

If nothing else, he felt pleased that when these two additional Masters arrived in the Low Hall, everyone now standing in positions that allowed Ned to hear everyone more clearly than before.

"—and have you sing us a lullaby," the Low Master said.

"What's a lullaby?" asked the Newcomer.

"A lullaby . . . Ah, yes, you wouldn't know, would you, coming as you do from the Lowland." He smiled slightly as he spoke.

"Perhaps she *does* know," said the Middle Choir's master. "Who knows what she or knows or doesn't? Prohibitions in the Lowland wouldn't necessarily stop some parents from—"

"Just tell me," Allu said, looking more and more impatient. "What's a lullaby? Is it some kind of music?"

"You don't know, do you?" asked the Low Master.

Allu shrugged. "Maybe I do," she said, "and maybe I don't. But if you won't explain yourselves, how can I know what you mean?"

Such rudeness, Ned told himself. This peasant would earn the Masters' wrath. Best to watch, listen, and leave quickly. How much did he want to associate with someone talking so impudently to the Masters? Ned had suffered enough disfavor already. It seemed obvious that any concern about the Newcomer could heighten the risk.

The Middle Master said, "Perhaps we should find out." With those words she turned to the Low Master's assistant who had been lingering a short distance away, and told her: "Listen closely. Alert all the Low Choir servants. Have nine of them go at once into the courtyard, locate a dozen young children—babies, toddlers, and a few others of slightly greater age—and bring them here. The parents will wait outside the hall. Quickly now!"

The gray-haired assistant hurried out of the room.

Ned couldn't even guess what was about to happen. Children? What children?

Just a short while later a scattering of servants returned to the hall. Three of them carried babies in their arms. Three led in boys and girls two or three years of age. Three brought older children. All of these youngsters looked restless and unhappy. The babies cried in the servants' arms. Some of the toddlers fussed, others wailed, and all of them resisted their captors by dragging their feet or trying to escape. Even two older children, each six or seven years old, whined and asked questions as the women led them in. The servants struggled to keep their charges under control and barely prevailed.

Observing this scene as it unfolded, Ned still didn't understand what the Master had in mind. What did these squalling children have to do with the Newcomer and her musical abilities? Were they taunting her in some way? Were they punishing the young woman for her impudence by subjecting her to an odd ordeal?

The Newcomer's expression showed perplexity and discomfort nearly equal to what Ned himself was feeling. She said nothing; she just stood there.

Raising his voice over the chorus of wails, whines, and screams, the Low Master told Allu, "A lullaby is a song for calming children. If it's good enough, it can put them to sleep. Do you know such a song?"

Allu gestured vaguely.

"Do you?"

"I don't know."

"Perhaps you've heard songs of this sort down there in the Low-land," said the other master, "even though such songs are forbidden?"

Allu shook her head.

The Middle Master said, "Don't be afraid. Don't be ashamed to tell us. This isn't the Lowland, is it? The rules are different here."

"How could a song calm a child?" Allu inquired abruptly. "I mean, how could just a simple song put a child to sleep?"

"Because the child would have no choice," replied the Low Master.

"No choice . . . ?"

"Perhaps you can imagine such a song, Allu. Even if you've heard nothing similar in the Lowland, perhaps you've heard one in your mind. Is that possible? Show us what you can do. Calm the children. Give them no choice but to fall asleep."

When Allu started to protest, the Low Master raised a hand to silence her.

She stood there for a long moment. Ned couldn't tell what she was thinking—whether she felt angry, discouraged, or defeated—only that she stayed still and silent.

The Masters, too, stood in silence. Noting an almost imperceptible glance between them, Ned expected that they would put an end to this pointless exercise and have the Newcomer taken away.

Then, without alerting anyone to what she intended, Allu began to sing:

> The mole in his burrow,
> The fox in her den,
> The worm in the furrow,
> The eel in the fen—

The melody unfolded, precise as a blossom. Listening, Ned felt his muscles relax and his mind ease much as he would have felt on sniffing the scent of a rose. All he wanted was to inhale the perfume. He didn't understand what was happening, but he didn't care. Only the song mattered.

> These creatures are weary;
> They all want to sleep—
> Sleep, sleep, sleep!
> Sleep, sleep, *sleeeeeep!*

She continued to sing, letting the melody grow as if sending out tendrils and buds that opened their petals to the light. As she sang, Ned noticed that the children before him—*changed*. The babies cried less urgently. The toddlers fussed less energetically. A little boy who had been struggling to escape from a servant's grip now stood calmly for a moment, then reached up until the young woman took him in her arms, and let him curl against her shoulder. A little girl who had been wailing inconsolably now sat on the floor and began to suck her thumb. Within a short while the noise diminished; the previously frantic motion of these children eased; and, to Ned's astonishment, the room fell silent.

This makes no sense, he thought. For a moment he couldn't recall where he was, and, glancing around, he couldn't remember who these people were, what they were doing, or why he was among them.

Without warning Ned felt so dizzy that he thought, *I have to sit.* He found a bench and sat abruptly. He imagined that the fire in the room must have been the fire back home, and his parents must have been nearby. Ned felt a deep longing for them. So many years had passed since he last saw them . . . But now he sat with them by the hearth, where he felt so safe and warm beside Mother and Father that he could doze off— Ned jolted upright and looked around in confusion.

Allu's song had ended.

The Masters stood a short distance away, observing Allu and smiling. What surprised him wasn't just that the previously fussy children had all fallen asleep, but that the servants attending them—the nine young women who had been holding the babies and toddlers—also rested calmly, looking dazed and sleepy.

As did most of the other adults in the room. The Master of the Low Choir. The Middle Master. The other master in her intricate robe. Only now did they start rousing back to awareness.

Finished singing, Allu asked: "Is that a lullaby?"

The Low Master grew sufficiently alert to answer this question. "That," he said, "is a lullaby."

11

The Masters' response to the Newcomer now seemed altogether different. They dismissed the servants, who left at once with the children in a squall of cries and squeals, their departure then allowing the masters to focus once more on Allu in the now-quiet hall. They clustered around her and, smiling, praised her for what she had accomplished.

"—so remarkable—"

"—would like to compliment you—"

"—nothing quite like you before—"

Although Ned couldn't follow all of these remarks, their tone was unmistakable. The Masters admired this girl and her song. They delighted in her abilities. They coveted something in her possession. Huddling around her—at times even reaching out to touch her, as if to confirm her being a real person, not just a wisp of their own wishful thinking—the Masters doted on her in ways that Ned had rarely observed in their behavior toward anyone else. He noted, however, that he himself had experienced something like this warm attention in the past. He had once been the object of deference and delight; had been treated with great warmth; had been the recipient of eager gazes; had once been—but was no longer.

What did they see in her? Granted, the Newcomer had calmed a dozen children. She had, in fact, put all of them to sleep. She had lulled most of the adults present in the same room. Doing so was remarkable; Ned himself had never witnessed anything of the sort. Why, however, did the Masters find this feat so astonishing? In what way did it foster the Realm's purposes? Surely the Masters had more crucial matters to consider than putting children to sleep! What struck them as so unusual about this Newcomer's actions? Baffled by these questions, Ned found it easy to feel pleased when the Masters finished speaking with the Lowlander and, to his surprise, dismissed her from their midst. The lass nodded awkwardly, took her leave, and walked out of the Low Hall.

At once he followed her.

Crossing paths with the Newcomer turned out easier than he had expected. He saw her proceeding this way and that, clearly unfamiliar with the maze of corridors in the Low Hall and thus baffled about where to go. She spoke with a few members of the Low Choir outside the hall, but, either misunderstanding or ignoring their advice, she didn't make much progress in leaving. Activities in progress throughout the area clearly distracted her: clusters of singers practicing their anthems in the hallways; fiddlers and pipers playing their instruments; drummers pounding intricately on their drums. Repeatedly Ned watched her stop and stare. At such times he, too, would stop, leaving ten or fifteen paces between himself and the Lowlander until she finished gawking. Then she would set off again, and he would follow.

She reached the Low Hall courtyard. This large space, paved with flat stones and graced with a large fountain in its center, was a favorite resting spot for members of the Low Choir. Now, as always, numerous singers stood or sat in the open area, where they either chatted, laughed and teased one another, or else sang together in twos and threes or in larger groups. The Lowland lass, keeping her distance from the gathered choristers by walking through the covered hallways along the courtyard's four sides, allowed Ned easy access: he simply crossed the courtyard and let his path intersect with hers at the far corner.

Approaching her, he sang his salutation: "All in harmony."

The Lowland girl turned and stared. After a moment's hesitation she asked, "Do I know you?"

He felt more disappointment than offense. She should have returned the proper salutation, of course, but that wasn't really what he sought; rather, he craved the sound of her voice singing the brief melody she should have used to greet him. He ignored his sense of letdown. He bowed. "My name is Nedettessi Jerosso," he told her, "and I am the First Order Apprentice to the Lord High Builder of Instruments. Please call me Ned."

"Ned," she stated, not responding so much as trying out the unfamiliar name.

"You are the Newcomer."

"I have just come here," she said, "so I suppose I must be new."

Was she taunting him? Ned wanted to find her words offensive, but the smile on her face suggested something other than wanting to give offense. "From Lari?"

She corrected him: "Laro."

"Forgive me—I know almost nothing about the Lowland."

"Perhaps the people here should know more about the Lowland," she told him, "since you're intent on holding sway over so many people." Speaking these words, she didn't even bother to soften them with a smile.

"Perhaps we should," he replied, "but it appears to be you who so easily holds sway over others."

Now the Newcomer looked uncertain. "What are you telling me?"

"I saw what you did back there in the Low Hall," Ned explained. "How you beguiled not only a dozen babes and children but more than a dozen adults as well. The Masters, even."

"That's what they asked me to do," said the Newcomer, speaking as flatly as someone might when describing the weather.

"And that's precisely what you did."

"They were pleased."

"They were indeed."

"I don't know why."

"Neither do I."

"Perhaps all the babies and children are restless in this strange city," she told him.

"Not just babies," Ned replied, "and not just children."

His comments appeared to make her even more uneasy. Changing the subject suddenly, she asked, "What was it you called yourself?"

He ignored her rudeness. "Ned."

"No, I mean your—title."

"First Order Apprentice to the Lord High Builder of Instruments."

"Builder of Instruments. Instruments being tools of some sort?"

"You might say that."

"My parents are ironsmiths," she told him, "and they work hard making hammers, pokers, shovels, hatchets, and axes."

Ned, grasping the girl's words, put them to his own use: "You might say that I, too, make tools—tools not for digging dirt or chopping wood but for making music."

"Tools for making music!" she said with a laugh.

He wanted to take offense at her amusement. But of course a Lowlander would know nothing of musical instruments, and rightly so, since all were forbidden. Having just arrived in Sifirithi, this girl would find the notion puzzling, baffling, even outrageous. He said, "By all means laugh. I know what I've said sounds preposterous."

"Instruments," she said again, still clearly amused.

"Such tools do exist. My honor is to make them. I study with the Lord High Builder—"

"A musical ironsmith!"

"—and he teaches me to build them," Ned continued, ignoring the interruption.

Looking more serious now, she said, "I've heard of such things. Once, in the Laro marketplace, I even saw someone play what must have been an instrument. But instruments seem so odd— So risky—" She cut the words short. "Surely the Masters wouldn't permit such devices."

"Why is that?"

"They are forbidden."

He started to understand her confusion. "They are forbidden," he told her, "except in Sifirithi. Here they are anything but forbidden. On the contrary, they are encouraged. My role—my honor—is to make as many instruments as possible."

"You make them . . . yourself?" she asked. Her expression showed a mix of confusion and curiosity, as if Ned had revealed where to find a hoard of buried treasure.

"Not entirely."

"The Lord High Builder you mentioned . . . This person helps you?"

"He guides me, teaches me, and inspires me. Then I do the actual work myself in my workshop."

Again a look eased onto her face: how intently she stared at him! Ned felt uncomfortable to be observed so eagerly, yet he felt delighted and relieved, too, after many days of seeing people avert their gaze when they saw him. He didn't know how to respond, her attention was so unfamiliar.

"Your workshop . . ." she echoed. "A workshop for making instruments . . ."

Not expecting the words he spoke next, Ned told her, "I could show you."

She looked uneasy.

"But only if you really want to see it," he added hastily.

A sudden smile. "Of course I would! Don't misunderstand! I just couldn't believe I would ever hear such an invitation."

Like clouds drifting across the sun, doubts darkened his thoughts. Was her visiting the workshop a good idea? Ned knew next to nothing about this Lowlander—only that her name was Allu, that she hailed from a town called Laro, that she had just arrived in Sifirithi, that she still lacked any rank or honor . . . and that she possessed the most beautiful voice imaginable. Ned's reputation, already damaged, might suffer additional harm if he allowed a mere Newcomer to visit. Perhaps showing her the workshop wasn't such a good idea after all. At least not yet. Better to wait until Ned had regained the Lord High Builder's confidence. "Well, then," he said, "I'm sure we can do so some day."

"Some day?" she asked, clearly disappointed.

"Some day soon."

His words appeared to ease her disappointment. "That's very kind of you."

"Not at all."

They stood there awkwardly for a while without speaking before Allu broke the silence: "I must return to the Low Hall."

"That would be best."

"Goodbye."

"That's not what we say here," he noted.

She snorted loudly as if at a joke, then turned to leave. "All in harmony," she sang.

He sang back to her: "All in harmony."

ASCENT

12

omeone woke Allu early the next morning. "Come, they are waiting," said one of the servants, an old woman, as she helped Allu out of bed. The servant moved gently, but her attire—warm outdoor clothes—caught Allu's attention at once and made her uneasy.

"Where are you taking me?" Before she could even ask about Dessina—couldn't they say goodbye?—the servant hurried Allu to leave. She felt a surge of concern. "My robes—"

"Your nightgown is enough. You will not need your old garments."

She grew alarmed. These people must have been throwing her out after all. Surely Allu's singing had enraged the Masters. The lullaby, perhaps . . . Now she would receive her punishment.

Instead of sending her away, however, the old woman led Allu through many corridors and hallways, all empty and cold at such an early hour, dark except for light from a few torches on the walls, until they reached the great portals through which Allu had entered the Low Tower almost a week earlier. There, dim in the shadows, the Low Master awaited them. Allu didn't recognize him at first. Then she heard the rustle and click of his robes and knew without any doubt who it was.

"Where are you taking me?" she asked.

"To a place where you will thrive. To a person who will help you more than than I can."

Although she had never liked this Master, Allu now feared leaving him. She pulled back when these people tried to lead her away.

"Do not be afraid," the old servant told her.

The Low Master said, "There is nothing more you can learn here.

There is nothing I can teach you. Come along, now. We shall take you to the Middle Choir, where the Middle Master awaits you."

Allu went along reluctantly. The Master and the servant led her down the steps descending from the Low Tower into the central part of Sifirithi, then guided her through still-silent streets. Then they ascended through alleyways and staircases that wound their way up one of the two mountains. No one spoke. Allu's fear soon warmed into excitement. As the light intensified around her—for dawn was already arriving—she could see the path ahead and the houses right and left, everything more and more radiant as Allu and her companions climbed higher. Rough rock gave way to increasingly fine masonry. The walls glowed with sunrise. When she looked up toward the summit, Allu's eyes hurt from all the light. Yet these sights startled her less than the sounds. Music flowed all around her. Allu recognized the chimes of Sifirithi—except that the chimes now rang even higher than before, clear and precise, like snowfall.

By the time the procession reached its goal halfway up the mountainside, Allu was gasping for breath. Her companions were, too. The old woman had begun to lag; even the Master had slowed.

They stopped near the door of a conical tower. Allu asked, "This place?"

The Master nodded, bracing himself against a huge iron door handle. "This," he told Allu, "is the Middle Choir. I judged you harshly, my child. I thought you were just a rough little peasant. You are nothing of the kind. You deserve the Middle Master. And here he is," the Low Master said as the door swung open, revealing a plump bearded man, somewhat older than the man who spoke, standing with some servants on the other side.

The Middle Master asked, "The girl from Laro?"

"Her name is Allu," said the Low Master.

Later, once settled into her new room, Allu received a visitor.

"Sorrik!" she cried out. Allu ran to embrace the emissary. For a moment she wouldn't let him talk; she just kept hugging him.

"Now, now," he said at last. "You have no need for comforting. You have done even better than I ever thought possible."

"Why am I here?" Allu asked abruptly.

"For the simple reason that you did so well. You sang. The Masters listened. All along I have known that you would prove yourself. My only surprise is that you have ascended so rapidly."

Allu showed off the new robes that the Middle Choir servants had brought her. She stopped short, letting the robes make a rustling sound like that of wind rushing through a wheatfield. "But—what will I do here?"

"Sing, of course."

"I want to stay with my friends."

"You will have friends here, too."

"Are there young people here?"

"Some, though not as many as in the Low Choir. You are unusual. You see, most members of the Middle Choir have spent many years ascending."

Allu fell silent. She observed the old emissary closely. His expression revealed the pride he felt toward her. Allu realized that if Sorrik approved of something, she would have no cause for worry. Allu had gained this fine room, more servants, and new clothes—all without loss of anything that mattered. She would still be able to sing. That was what mattered most.

"The Middle Choir—what do they sing here?"

Sorrik hesitated. "Whatever the Master asks of you. Anthems, mostly. You will learn far more than you would have in the Low Choir."

Allu wanted him to explain. She worried about having to sing more tedious exercises. Since everyone had acted so oddly whenever she objected, however, she said nothing more.

"You will sing what you need to sing," Sorrik told her. "You will learn what you need to learn. The Middle Choir is a great honor, believe me. I am pleased with you. You will serve Sifirithi and the Harmonor even better than any of us imagined."

Allu didn't know what Sorrik meant, but he refused to explain further. They spoke for a while longer; then the old man left. Once again Allu felt frightened. She forced herself not to worry: everything was getting better, not worse. She would have time to ask more questions at another time.

Allu took part in the Middle Choir with great eagerness. She went to lessons and practice sessions in the Choir itself. Unlike the Low Choir, however, the Middle was small, not much more than two dozen members. Most of them looked older than Allu—late twenties or thirties in age, a few even in their forties. Unlike the Low Choristers, the members of this group seemed quiet, orderly, without any of the shoving and shouting that had wearied Allu before. Better yet, the students treated the newcomer gently. Even the Master seemed attentive and kind. Allu did what she was asked, she sang well, and she sought the plump Middle Master's assistance and approval.

"We shall now sing the Anthem for Calming the Fearful," said the Master, "since we made such good progress yesterday. He waited for his students to be ready.

Allu turned to one of them nearby—a woman with pure black hair and eyes almost as dark—and she asked, "The Anthem for what?"

The woman said, "Please, we are starting now."

"I don't understand."

"We are about to start."

At that moment the Choir began to sing.

Allu only listened. The melody rose from all around her, almost too quiet to hear at first, then louder. Allu wanted to cry out: this sounded like the dull Low Choir exercises. Then she realized that the music was different—far different—and within a few moments, she started laughing with delight. Tunes rose from the Choir like vines reaching out for the light. Allu listened a while longer, then joined in without either wanting or not wanting to sing.

She learned fast. She pleased the Master. She made friends with the other choristers. She surprised everyone that such a young woman could sing so easily and so well. Allu worked hard because she wanted to prove herself to these people, but also because she simply liked to sing. Unlike the Low Choir exercises, these Middle Choir Anthems pleased her. She liked their melodies. They felt good when she sang them—rich and warm in her throat. Everything felt safe and good as she sang, and the feelings of safety and goodness lingered for a long time afterwards.

When she mentioned to the Master how she felt, he laughed at her gently. "Of course you feel good. What do you think these anthems are for?"

"Oh, I don't know," Allu replied. "I didn't think they were for anything."

His bald brow wrinkled and his lips pursed. The Master observed her closely. "No?" he said at last. "Do you imagine we sing simply for amusement? For fun? For nothing?"

"I suppose there must be a purpose."

"These anthems exist for the good of Siir and the good of Sifirithi. Please don't forget that."

"I promise."

The Master watched Allu for a while. He looked uncomfortable, as if that gloomy expression didn't fit his face. Allu laughed at him. Then he, too, laughed. "You are a fine one!" he said. "I would be tempted to worry about you, but you never give me a chance. So young yet so clever! You surely won't forget the good of Sifirithi. I daresay, too, you have more good to offer than all my other students combined."

She asked, "What do you mean? What good? All I do is sing."

"That," said the Master, "is precisely how you offer it."

"But how? Tell me."

"Soon enough you will have no need for me—or anyone—to explain."

13

One afternoon, when the Master let the Middle Choristers take a day off to do whatever they pleased, Allu left the Middle Tower and walked down into the low part of Sifirithi. She liked going off to explore. Back home in Laro, her whole life was an ordeal of errands and chores. The Low Choir hadn't been much different, although musical chores made more sense than other kinds. Allu had never before had any time to herself. The Middle Choir gave her the first chance, and now Allu took advantage of her new freedom.

She liked the city. Orderly and calm, its houses spread out between the three mountains and rose toward their summits. Windows glinted in the sunlight, making all of Sifirithi radiant. The chimes rang from the walls, eaves, and roofs until the wind itself became music. Allu wandered, looking and listening, amazed that such a place could exist, and amazed too that a mere villager like her could be living here.

The people surprised Allu even more than the place itself. She had always believed the stories about Sifirithi and its people: their cruelty, their greed, their treachery. Now she didn't know what to think. People went out of their way to greet her, sometimes even crossing the street to draw closer. Others waved from a distance. Still others called out.

"Welcome!" an old woman shouted from her balcony. "All in harmony! Are you one of the Song Guards?"

Two men yelled, "Hail to the Song Guards!"

Some little boys echoed them: "Hail! Hail!"

Allu passed among them feeling surprised but also pleased. She waved to the people who greeted her. Proceeding cautiously, she kept on her way without stopping, yet nothing could have delighted her more than these cordial salutations.

She ended up in the Great Circle, a big grassy area surrounded by curved, step-like terraces, where children played and adults stood around in small groups. Allu hesitated for a moment before going further, as she thought everyone might swarm around her. Then she realized why that wouldn't happen: some of the Low Choir singers had come here, too, and nobody seemed to bother them. Allu went ahead, found a place to sit, and made herself comfortable on the grass.

"Allu! Here you are!" someone called out just then.

Startled, Allu looked up.

Dessina waved to Allu from across the Circle, then came striding closer.

Allu stood to greet her companion.

When they embraced, Dessina hung on tightly. She said, "I thought you were gone! I was worried about you!"

"I left when you were asleep. The Master came for me. I wanted to say goodbye, but he wouldn't let me."

"Came for you? And took you where?"

"To the Middle Choir."

Now Dessina pulled back. "They *what?*"

"Took me to the Middle Choir."

Dessina stared at Allu. "You were with us only a few days. How could you leave so soon?"

Allu shook her head. "I didn't understand, either, but that's what they did."

Now a strange look came over Dessina's face: a tight expression. She stared at Allu without blinking. "I came to the Low Choir almost a year ago. Some of the others have been there even longer. Why should you go to the Middle Choir after just a few days?"

"I don't know."

"What did you do to gain such special treatment?"

"Nothing. Not a thing." Allu began to feel afraid. She saw Dessina starting to tremble, though not from fear. Allu said, "It wasn't anything I did. The Masters made the decision—for the good of Sifirithi."

"What's so good about you that isn't good about me? Tell me that."

Some of the people nearby in the Circle started noticing the young women's tense words. A few now gathered around Allu and Dessina.

Allu's fright kept her from escaping. Then fright turned to sadness, for this argument would surely end her time in Sifirithi.

She remembered the anthems. Dessina's shouts distracted her for a moment: she couldn't concentrate with all that noise. When she recalled something that the Middle Choir had practiced recently—the Anthem for Subduing Envy and Spite—she took a deep breath and started singing.

> Envy spreads like flames within your flesh.
> Spite explodes into a conflagration.
> Quench this fire! Quench this fire!

Dessina stopped shouting almost at once. The expression on her face resembled that of someone splashed with cold water. Dessina glanced this way and that, her mouth a small O. Allu wanted to laugh at her. She couldn't stop singing, however, and she didn't. She sang. The anthem filled the air. The melody caught hold of Dessina and wouldn't let her escape. She stood there, frowning at first, then neither frowning nor smiling, then smiling.

> Quench this fire! Quench this fire!

Allu sang for a while longer. The people around her watched and waited. They, too, started smiling. Then Allu stopped. She wasn't sure whether to keep singing, but she stopped anyway.

For a moment there was no other music but the chimes of Sifirithi. Then Dessina said, "Forgive me, Allu. I was mistaken. Forgive me."

Now Allu understood. No one would ever scold her again. No one would belittle or punish her. No one would make her do anything that Allu herself chose not to do. She understood, too, that this situation would happen because Allu made it happen. Best of all, she would have her way without anyone minding. She wouldn't force anyone to do anything: people would want what Allu herself wanted. She would help them want it. Then she would have her way.

Everyone would be happy.

≈   ≈   ≈

Allu felt astonished to find that right after this incident, Dessina be-
haved as if no conflict had occurred between them. She didn't even
seem to recall the argument. They set off to explore the city. And as
they walked through the streets and alleyways, Dessina said amiably.
"—and something good has happened."

"Yes?" Allu inquired.

"I'm about to get married."

"How exciting!" Allu felt surprised to hear this sudden news but
glad for Dessina's sake and especially pleased to be avoiding any further discussion of the Middle Choir. "Who's the lucky lad?"

"A Lowlander like you, though he's lived a long time here in Sifirithi. He's very handsome and greatly gifted!"

"Wonderful!"

"He has been through tough times lately, but I'm sure he'll come
through everything, and—" Dessina interrupted herself.

Rounding the corner, they stopped short. A crowd of fifteen or
twenty people blocked their path through the narrow street.

"What's happening?" Allu asked.

"I'm not sure."

A woman approached from the left just then, shoving her way
among the people in the street. As the crowd parted, Allu caught sight
of what this woman was struggling so frantically to reach: a man lying
face up on the cobblestones. The woman rushed over to him, knelt,
and began to wail. "No!" she cried. "No, no—please! No!" She clung
to the man and sobbed.

Easing closer to get a better look, Allu saw an appalling sight. A
long wooden ladder lay diagonally in the street. A bucket and a brush
rested near a long splash of white paint on the cobblestones. The
man, his right leg twisted beneath him and his arms thrown outward,
his palms open, stared sightless at the sky. Blood trickled from his
ears. The woman beside him stroked his brow and cried out harshly,
panting and whimpering like a dog.

Allu felt sick as she viewed this scene. She wanted to turn and leave.
Nothing she could do would help this broken, dying man. At the same

time, she couldn't stop staring at the sight of him lying in the street.

One of the other bystanders shouted, "Summon the Healers!"

A woman's voice echoed him: "The Healers!"

"Can't anyone help him?" Allu asked Dessina. Even back home in a poor town like Laro, someone would have offered assistance. The village apothecary would have arrived with his vials of medicine. The physician would have showed up with her satchel of poultices and oils. Someone—

Without warning the knot of bystanders untied itself, the crowd backed off, and seven or eight men and women strode into the intersection. Wearing red-and-black robes whose pattern Allu didn't recognize, they arrived abruptly, lined up in a row, and began to sing.

> Mend yourselves, O broken bones!
> Knit yourself, O flesh!
> Stanch your wayward flow, O blood!

"Tell me what's happening," Allu stated quietly to Dessina.

"These are the Healers," she replied. "They've come to help this injured man."

The Healers! Allu couldn't believe what she was witnessing. Before her lay a twisted, bleeding body, yet all these Healers offered him was a song! She would have laughed out loud if the sight hadn't been so awful.

Without a word she turned and left the crowd.

Dessina caught up with her a moment later, asking, "What's the matter?"

"I couldn't watch."

"It's upsetting—such a terrible accident."

"Made worse by an ugly song."

"Pardon me?" Dessina looked uncertain.

"As if it's not sad enough that the man suffered a fall," Allu said, her voice tight with disgust, "now he—and his wife, too!—have to suffer through the Healers' song. Healers, indeed!"

"But they *are* healers," Dessina told her.

"Please spare me."

Striding through the city, Allu walked so fast that Dessina could scarcely keep up with her.

Dessina said, "The Healers will do just that. Will heal the man. Far from suffering because of their song, as you put it, the man will benefit. Will be healed."

"Because he heard some notes?"

"Because he heard the Anthem to Mend Fractures. The Anthem to Heal Dire Wounds. The Anthem—"

"Do you consider me such a fool," Allu asked, stopping so abruptly that Dessina nearly collided with her, "that you think I'll believe what you're telling me? That these songs will heal a man who fell more than three times his height? Who crashed onto the cobblestones and smashed his skull?"

Dessina gestured awkwardly. "I don't consider you a fool," she replied, "and you can believe whatever you wish. The fact remains: the Healers heal the injured and the sick. The anthems are powerful. The man who fell has suffered great harm. I can't promise he will recover fully from his accident. I believe you'll see him again, however, and if so, you can speak with him. Ask him how he's doing. You'll learn a thing or two about what the Healers can accomplish."

"I'm sure I will," Allu said before turning and walking off again, faster now than before.

14

What, exactly, had she witnessed? What had happened after the man fell and the Healers assisted him? How could the Healers' songs be so powerful? How could a grievously injured man benefit just because some people sang to him? Allu pondered this situation and tried to make sense of it. She felt confused, uneasy, and intrigued.

At the same time, she realized that despite her confusion and unease, she now felt happier than at any other time in her life. Not only did she have what she wanted—the freedom to sing—but the people here *wanted* her to have it. She could scarcely believe her good fortune. Allu had attained more than she had ever thought possible back in Laro. Still more surprising, even the Master spoke of how much she offered.

Days passed. Allu studied and took part in the Middle Choir. Everything went well.

Almost everything.

One thing troubled her: Allu's own songs came to her less often than before. Sometimes, mostly at night, Allu heard the voices that previously arrived so often, drenched her with music like a storm, and left her shaking. Yet the voices came to her so rarely now that she couldn't help but wonder why. What had changed? What had gone wrong? Sometimes Allu waited for a long time before going to sleep in hopes that the dreamsongs would return. Perhaps those voices wanted all other sounds in her head to leave before they drew near again. Perhaps they would come only if she listened with full attention. Allu didn't know what to think. When they did return—always suddenly— she often cried out for joy. But the exhaustion afterwards, the dizziness, the fear: maybe those voices weren't such a good thing after all.

Better, she decided, to have a voice she could control. Better to focus on her studies, which were enough, surely, to keep her occupied.

Something else. Or, more accurately, someone. Ned. Where was he? What was he doing? She wondered about him for a while, then wondered why she was wondering.

She decided on impulse to go find him. Leaving the Low Hall, Allu wandered through the city for a while, uncertain how to locate someone in such a large, crowded place. Then she decided simply to ask for help. "Can you tell me where to find Nedettesi Jerosso?" she asked a woman near the largest of the town squares. "Ned, the builder of instruments?"

"Ned Jerosso? Up there," the woman told her, motioning toward one of the three hillsides that loomed over the city's central area.

"Thank you!"

"Though if it's instruments you want . . ." Letting her words trail into silence, the woman turned and walked away.

Allu echoed these words: "If it's instruments I want . . ." Since there was no response, however, Allu could only watch the woman cross the square and vanish into the crowd.

Allu headed off in the opposite direction. She soon found herself striding up a steeply angled street and, a short while later, climbing a series of stone staircases built into the hillside.

She stopped now and then to catch her breath and take in the changing view. She also asked for directions from people she encountered: "Can you direct me to the dwelling of Ned Jerosso?"

People invariably stopped to help her. They pointed to a nearby alleyway between the houses that fitted together as tightly as stones in a wall, they gave her instructions—"Turn left here, walk to the next street, then turn right and continue upward"—and they sometimes even guided her themselves for a while before stating, "Now just keep going." They always responded to her request with a friendly chuckle. Allu felt pleased that everyone here seemed to know Ned.

Would she have to climb the whole mountain? Dizzy and heaving for breath, Allu couldn't help wondering as she clambered up one staircase after another. How did these people tolerate living in such a steep place? They might as well have been mountain goats, living like this! Yet when she turned to face outward, she caught sight of the city now spread out below—not just the saddle-like area between the peaks, but the mountainsides themselves, two of them covered with stone buildings, the third and tallest peak bare of buildings except for a cluster at the summit—and Allu couldn't help but find the sight stirring and impressive. Standing so high on a steep slope left her dazed, however, and at times she worried that she would grow faint, stumble, and fall.

"All in harmony," someone sang to her.

She turned to see a boy perhaps seven or eight years old staring at her. She sang back: "All in harmony."

Noticing her Middle Choir robes and unfamiliar face, he asked, "Who are you—and what are you doing here?"

"My name is Allu," she told him, "and I'm looking for Ned Jerosso."

"Ned Jerosso!" He sounded surprised, even amused.

"The builder of instruments." For good measure she added: "The extraordinary builder of instruments."

Now the boy laughed outright. "Extraordinary? He's not even *ordinary!* He's the *worst!*"

"What are you saying?" asked Allu, shocked by this outburst.

"My parents say he's the worst ever!"

She flustered as she heard these words. What right did this child have to mock someone like Ned? Startling herself as well as the boy, she blurted, "You little fool—"

"*He's* the fool!" he shouted.

"Oh, stop it!"

Windows overlooking the alleyway started to open as people stuck their heads out to investigate the commotion. Someone called out, "What's the matter?"

Uneasy, Allu looked up. Seven or eight people were now staring at her from above and across the street. "What's happening?" asked a woman at the same moment a man shouted, "Cease all this noise!"

She couldn't decide whether to respond, ignore them, or simply leave.

"Allu!"

Now she glanced around. Who was calling her name?

"Allu!"

She was astonished to see an open doorway just a few paces up the street and, standing near it, Ned Jerosso.

He motioned to her.

Allu walked the short distance necessary to reach him. He stood before a narrow oak door angled inward to reveal a wooden staircase beyond. "Ned."

"Why are you here?" he demanded, clearly uncomfortable with her presence.

"To find you."

"Me?"

"To see your instruments."

Overhearing this exchange, the little boy called out: "He's the worst!"

"Shut up, you little brat!" Allu shouted suddenly. She cut herself short at once. What was she doing, lashing out at a mere child! Then at once she yelled again anyway: "What do you know about instruments! You couldn't build an instrument to save your life!"

At once all the people leaning out of windows started shouting back: "Go away!" "Leave, Newcomer!" and "Leave at once, or we'll summon the Song Guards!"

"Get inside," Ned told Allu.

She hesitated. "I just want to speak with you—"

"Then get in here," he said. "Now."

Listening to all the commotion at her back, Allu hesitated for a moment, then obeyed him.

The silence inside Ned's house calmed her. She followed him up the staircase, their footsteps on the stone steps the only sound. In the meager light she worried about tripping, but they soon reached an open doorway and stepped into a well-lit room.

Nothing she had imagined could have prepared Allu for what she saw before her now. Her parents' iron workshop had always seemed big to her, with its furnace, bellows, anvils, and racks of hammers and tongs. By comparison, Ned's workshop extended wider and deeper, contained far more benches, shelves, and stockpiles of materials, and, most impressively of all, ended in a row of tall windows that looked out over the city. Allu walked over to those windows and stared at the view for a long time. Then, on impulse, she unlatched and opened the window closest to her. At once two or three different melodies wafted toward her from the chimes arrayed all around.

Ned watched her but said nothing.

Then she closed the window, latched it, and turned. She walked over to the nearest workbench and, picking up a box-like device with holes drilled into it, asked, "This is an instrument?"

"Everything here is an instrument," Ned told her, "or else something that will some day become one. And each will play music."

Allu saw racks of metal, wood, cloth, wire, glass . . . "That makes no sense," she said bluntly. "How can these things make music?"

"There is music inside everything," Ned replied. "The task is to coax it out."

"I don't know what you mean," Allu told him.

She expected him to argue, but he didn't. He simply walked over to where she stood, reached over to a nearby rack, and picked up a stick. "What is this?"

"A stick," Allu answered.

"No—it's a musical instrument."

"Some instrument!" she exclaimed with a laugh.

"True indeed." He held the stick out, whipping it through the air, making a windy note.

Allu laughed at him again. "Convincing me will take more than that."

Without speaking further, Ned picked up a knife in his right hand, held the stick in his left, and trimmed away some little twigs that branched out from the shaft. Then he tapped the stick against the wall that rose beside them. It made a gentle sound, not quite but almost musical, halfway between a click and a tone.

Allu listened, amused but not impressed. "So?"

Ned used his knife to trim away part of the tip, enough that when he tapped the stick against the table again, the tone was higher than before. "Even a stick wants to sing," he said. "There's music hiding there." He tapped the stick again. "All we have to do is find it."

She repeated his words: "All we have to do is find it."

Ned walked over to a row of ten or twelve glass goblets arrayed on a table. Allu noticed that some were small, some intermediate in size, and some much larger. Watching, she saw Ned lick his index finger; then he rubbed the rim of the smallest goblet. A low tone emerged, surprising her. Ned rubbed the next largest cup. Once again a tone came forth, higher now. He proceeded to touch several of the other rims, and with each stroke he produced a different tone, clear as a human voice.

"These goblets, too, are full of music," Ned told her. "Music that wants to emerge so we can hear it."

Finishing this demonstration, he gazed at Allu. The intensity and duration of his unwavering gaze puzzled her from the start and soon made her uneasy. She had no idea what he might be thinking. She couldn't imagine what he might do or say. Would he tell her that their time together had now ended? Would he ask her to leave? "I want to show you something," he said. With those words he crossed the room, approached a cabinet, opened a drawer, and began rummaging among the objects inside. His hand emerged with a ring of keys—the ring wider than Allu's hand, the iron keys longer than her fingers. "Come with me."

She followed him to the doorway, out into the landing, and up a flight of stone stairs. Rather than stopping at the next floor, however, Ned proceeded still higher. Two flights, three. They arrived at the top floor. Before them stood a large oak door crossed with black iron braces.

Ned inserted a key into the lock. The lock tolerated the key at first, then resisted, grinding and rattling like a dog gnawing on a stick. Ned struggled, relented, and struggled again. He said, "It's sick with rust."

Wincing at the harsh noise, Allu cupped both hands against her head to shield her ears.

Then, just as Ned seemed ready to give up, the key turned. The lock clanked. He smiled at Allu. "We're in." Ned grabbed the handle, twisted, and pulled. The great oak door swung open. Even by opening, however, this door warned the intruders to keep their distance, for the hinges squealed more hideously than a pig succumbing to a butcher's knife. Allu hesitated, appalled by the noise. The shrillness wasn't what alarmed her; rather, she worried that the rusty cry would alert someone in the area—the Song Guards, perhaps—and bring them running. She backed off.

"Come," Ned told her, reaching out.

"We mustn't." She glanced down the stairway.

"There's nothing to fear." He sounded so confident, so unafraid. "As a builder of instruments, I have access to this place."

Although the door now fell mute, Allu still expected the Song Guards to have heard the door's noise and to come clattering up the stairs. Nothing announced anyone's approach, however. Nothing even hinted at anyone's awareness of Ned and Allu. The stairs, the landing, and the room beyond the doorway lay steeped in silence. The only sound came from the wind's warble against a window.

Ned motioned for Allu to go ahead.

Though unsure and afraid, she went in anyway.

The room was far bigger than she had anticipated. Its walls curved away from her as if boasting of their breadth, and they rose to form the highest ceiling Allu had ever seen. Slit-like windows let great blades of sunlight stab through the walls and cleave the air. Even the High Choir's hall would have looked paltry by comparison. Allu took only a few paces before she faltered, and for a long time she merely stared at the vast vault before her. Allowing her gaze to descend from the room's upper reaches, Allu started noticing what lay ahead of her. Tables. Long wooden tables. Ten, fifteen, perhaps twenty such tables, some against the walls and some lined up in rows within the room itself. And on the tables—

"What am I looking at?" she asked, at once helpless and eager.

Ned motioned once again. "Come and see."

Allu proceeded carefully. The more she gazed at the room's

contents, the less she understood what she saw. Objects covered the tables, but objects of what sort? Tools? Weapons? Farm implements? Nothing looked familiar. The sheer variety of devices, too, confused her: none of the items arrayed on the tables resembled any of the others. Some were long, some short. Some looked barrel-like, some boxy, some flat, some tube-shaped. Some appeared to be made of metal, others of wood, still others of stone or animal hide. Allu let her vision wander across the expanse of all these things, and she tried hard to make sense of what her eyes showed her, yet ultimately what she saw left her struggling, helpless and bewildered, as if awash in a rising tide that threatened to sweep her away.

"I don't understand," she stated, suddenly running both hands through her hair. "What are you showing me?"

Ned strode over to the nearest stable and picked up the object lying closest to where he stood. If it bore any resemblance to something within Allu's own experience, then it resembled a paddle of the kind that fisherfolk in Laro use to propel their boats: broad at the end but tapered to form a long, narrow handle. Yet this wasn't a paddle—Allu saw that right away. The wide part was hollow, and some cords or threads extended from the wide end almost to the handle. Was it a loom, then? Some kind of small loom? Allu's efforts to make sense of this device left her more and more confused.

She told him, "Explain what you're showing me."

Ned's only answer was to run his fingers sideways across the cords. At once an odd series of sounds unwound, as faint and wispy as the dust that rose simultaneously with them into the air.

"A loom for music," Allu said, at once puzzled and astonished.

Ned laughed at her gently. "Not loom," he said. "Lute."

"Lute?"

"It's an instrument."

She felt more confused, not less so. "I still don't understand what you'e saying."

Cradling the lute in his left arm, Ned caressed the cords with all the gentleness of a father soothing his baby. "It's a device for playing music." More notes rose, wafted into the air, and dispersed.

"And this one?" she asked, picking up a polished wooden tube with a line of holes bored into the shaft.

"It's called a flute," Ned told her.

"Flute," Allu said, trying out the word for size.

Ned took it from her, blew across it, and produced a fluttery noise that resembled the wind nudging tree branches. When he placed his fingertips on the flute's holes, the noise fell or rose.

"This one?" asked Allu. She lifted a strange contraption from the table. It consisted of a leather pouch roughly the size, shape, and texture of a wineskin; three floppy wooden tubes; and a longer tube which, like the flute still in Ned's hands, had been pierced with a line of holes.

Once again Ned took what she handed him. "It's called a bagpipe," he said. "It works a bit like the flute, though the bag does some of the work." Squeezing it, the bag made a sound that reminded Allu of a dog whining in its sleep.

Allu gazed over the wild array of devices on the tables before her. "These are all—instruments?"

"These," Ned echoed, "are instruments."

She felt a surge of bewilderment. "But why?"

"Why what?" Ned looked confused.

"Why do they exist?"

"Well—" He faltered. "They exist because someone built them."

Shaking her head, Allu brushed her hand across the lute's strings. "That makes no sense. It's like saying a cat is a cat because it was born."

"I don't know why someone built them, if that's what you mean," Ned told her. "Much less do I know how to play them. Not well, anyway. All I know is that someone built them long ago and surely played them. No one plays them any longer. Now, many years later, here they are."

"All locked up."

"Of course."

"Why of course?" she asked.

"Because they're dangerous."

"Dangerous!"

"What could be more dangerous than musical instruments in the wrong hands? There's no telling what people might do if they gained access to this armory."

"You do."

Ned looked uncertain.

"You have access," she clarified.

"Yes—but for a purpose. Building instruments is my duty and my honor," Ned told her. "I come here to study these instruments, to make sense of them, to adapt what I learn to my own inventions." He picked up the flute again. Blowing across the tip, he released a tone, then used his fingertips to cover or uncover the holes that lined up along the instrument's shaft. A melody emerged from the flute like fragrant steam rising from a teapot.

Listening, Allu didn't understand what was happening to her. The back of her neck felt hot, yet she shivered—just once but suddenly and hard. Some kind of dizziness came over her. She started to breathe faster and more deeply. Her eyes welled up. A single tear eased down her left cheek. She had never imagined such an odd device or such music springing out of it. What was this music? What was it doing to her?

Most baffling was how Ned's music prompted music of her own—prompted a dreamsong to rise from deep within her, and, filling her body and her mind, prompted her to sing.

> I am here, you are there, and now we stand
> Not knowing what we think at all.

Where did that tune come from? What did the words mean? She didn't know. But Ned and Allu made music anyway, their melodies completely different yet somehow combining into one substance. The effort of singing and playing required no effort at all, was no more strenuous than floating together in a warm lake. They gazed at each other, smiling, sharing their astonishment and delight.

Ned stopped abruptly. He set the flute on the table with a loud clack. He glanced at Allu, then away.

"What's the matter?" she asked.

"We mustn't."

"Mustn't what?" She stared at him, examined his tense expression, tried to make sense of it.

"Mustn't."

Sadness welled up inside her. "It was beautiful. It was—perfect."

He told her, "It is forbidden."

"What is forbidden?" Allu asked in bafflement.

"The music. What we created."

"Forbidden," she stated in a flat tone, examining the word as she might examine a dead insect she had crushed with her foot, then had picked up to examine. "Such a harmless thing, forbidden? Were we hurting anyone? Were we depriving anyone of anything? Your words make no sense."

Ned now rearranged some of the instruments on the table. Watching, Allu saw with astonishment that he now handled these various devices as if they were hot to the touch. Hot—or unclean. He even wiped both hands on his robe as he finished. "It doesn't need to make sense," he told her. "All that matters is that the Masters haven't sanctioned this music—haven't permitted it—and thus it is forbidden."

With those words he turned and walked out of the room.

VI

RUMORS AND PREPARATIONS

15

O nce Allu left—which Ned insisted must happen at once—he sat alone in his workshop. The room's silence soothed him like cool water on a hot day. He felt pleased to have her gone. More than pleased: relieved. What could Allu have been thinking? To sing without permission! Worse yet, to sing a strange song that couldn't possibly have been sanctioned. Worst of all, to coax Ned into joining her, collaborating with her, and offering an accompaniment on an instrument that the Lord High Builder hadn't yet allowed him to use. What could Ned have been thinking?

What disturbed him most of all was the beauty of Allu's song. Of her singing. Of her voice. Of—

He forced his mind elsewhere. Enough of Allu!

His thoughts turned at once to the Lord High Builder. A messenger had arrived just yesterday to request Ned's appearance. Ned was to present himself at his Master's workshop for another discussion. Today. How unusual: such meetings ordinarily took place only once a month. One had occurred just a few days earlier. Why was the Master calling him back so soon? Not a good development! Perhaps the High Builder had changed his mind about the recent calamity and would now subject Ned to further criticism after all. Why else would he order this visit? Thinking over the situation, Ned felt deep concern. Alarm. Dread. Yet failure to comply—even failure to arrive precisely on time—would heap firewood on what might already be the crackling flames of the High Builder's contempt and anger.

All the more reason, then, for Ned's astonishment when he found his Master not only cordial but warm.

"All in harmony," he sang to Ned upon arrival.

"All in harmony."

"You are well, I hope?"

"Just fine, Master," Ned replied. "And you?"

"Very well indeed." The Master's thick beard and mustache, some of whose whiskers spread sideways from his cheeks, made him look like a contented cat.

"That pleases me." After hesitating a moment, Ned took the risk of adding, "I've been worried, however, that you feel anger toward me after all."

The High Builder couldn't suppress a laugh. "Angry? On the contrary, I'm pleased to see you. We have much to discuss. Let's put the past behind us. What interests me is the future."

"Which future do you mean?"

"Which future!"—another laugh. "Yours!"

"I wasn't sure I had one," Ned told him.

"Don't be daft. Of course you do. Let's not waste time with this silliness. We have important matters at hand." The High Builder now eased out of the chair next to his workbench and stepped over to the nearby wood stove. He filled a pot with water and placed it on the stovetop. Preparing tea in two cups, he continued. "You may or may not know about the troubles this realm is facing. Troubles in the Lowland. Restlessness among the peasantry. Lack of cooperation. Refusal to provide the animals and the crops people owe as tribute. Mind you, most of the peasants down there behave well enough, obey the laws, and cause no problems. We mustn't find fault with all of them. A few, however—more than a few—are a dilemma that appears to be spreading. There have been outbreaks of violence. When the Song Guards suppressed the troublemakers recently, other Lowlanders lashed back. The situation has grown worse, not better."

Ned, listening to the High Builder's commentary, nodded out of genuine concern. "How much worse?" He felt a sudden, deep twinge of worry about his parents' safety.

"Bad enough that certain Lowland factions have stolen wheat, barley, and farm animals destined for shipment to Sifirithi. Abundant supplies are now missing. Enough supplies to reduce the amount of food available to us over the next several weeks. Oh, don't be alarmed!" said the Master, noticing signs of worry in Ned's expression. "No one will go hungry. There will be enough to eat. You can surely grasp, however, why this situation prompts concern. Concern and—outrage. These Lowlanders have no right to take what belongs to the Realm! They must offer tribute to Sifirithi. Above all, to the Harmonor. Do various quantities of wheat, barley, and corn make a big difference? Do a few dozen goats and pigs? Not really. But if these troublemakers decide to steal animals and crops today, what crimes will they commit tomorrow?"

"One can only guess."

"Indeed. So, as you can imagine, they must be stopped. More than stopped: punished. More than punished: halted in such a way that other Lowlanders fully grasp that obedience is paramount, that these outrages against the Realm are intolerable."

At this point Ned, though troubled by these words, felt confusion spread through his mind. "I need to ask you, Master, what this situation has to do with me."

The High Builder reached out and rested his right hand on Ned's left shoulder. "That is precisely what I'll explain. The answer is simple: everything."

Ned shook his head in bafflement.

"As we've discussed," the Master told him, "the current situation is unacceptable. It must stop at once. There's no question, however, that the Song Guards have proved less than effective in controlling these unruly Lowlanders—these traitors against the Realm. I don't mean to sound critical: the Song Guards have made valiant efforts. But so many peasants have caused so many problems that the Guards have failed to regain control. Their failure encourages the Lowlanders. For this reason, the Harmonor has asked some of the Masters to find other means."

"Means?"

"Of taking control. Of forcing obediance upon the traitors. Forcing as one forces a wild dog to submit."

"I still don't understand how—"

"Lad, you will provide the means."

"But how?" Ned asked in astonishment.

"By designing instruments whose music restrains the thieves' thievery and ends the traitors' treason."

Ned felt a flicker of delight realizing that the Lord High Builder would honor him so deeply; at the same time, this honor would be a burden. He gestured awkwardly. "How can I—"

"I know what you'll say," the Lord High Builder stated before Ned could express the worries now flooding his mind. "You have no idea what such instruments might be. No idea how they might control the Lowlanders. No idea how they will function or what they will sound like. And so forth. Of course you don't! Trust me: that's not a problem. The other Masters and I—even the Harmonor—all understand that you don't know yet. We're assigning you this mission not because you know, but because you'll find out. You'll perform experiments. You'll explore possibilities. You'll test materials, see what works, find out what doesn't. In doing so, you'll invent new instruments. Some will fail, of course. So be it. We trust that in a brief time you'll solve the problem and create precisely what we need.

"But the Avian Calliope—"

"Forget the Avian Calliope! Yes, it was a failure! Ned: it was a failure so grand, so spectacular, that only someone possessing your extraordinary gifts could have caused it. No one else would even have made the attempt! Your failures are much more interesting, more impressive, more promising, than most builders' successes. The Avian Calliope is long-past history. Pay no attention to what's past. What matters is what's happening now. What's happening now is this new mission."

"Master—"

"You'll have whatever you need—a new workshop, the best materials, a team of assistants. Anything you want."

"I'm not so sure—"

"Of course you're not. You're full of doubts. Very well, then. Put those doubts to work. Harness them like the carriers who lift our coaches and carry us so confidently to our destinations."

"Master—"

"There's nothing more to discuss. Go forth now. Start at once. By tomorrow morning I want a message from you listing whatever materials and equipment you want. Anything. Everything."

Leaving the High Builder's workshop and walking down toward the Great Circle, Ned found himself caught in a dizzying swirl of emotions. Relief, fear, pride, exhilaration, eagerness, dread: this whirlpool would drag him to the bottom of the sea. How strange and wonderful that despite his having failed so recently and so completely, the High Builder would now grant Ned this remarkable assignment. A difficult assignment, truly, but one that would prove fascinating and worthwhile. To defend the realm against thieving rebels! Against traitors! If Ned succeeded at his task, he would not only serve the people of Siir, the Masters who guids them, and, indeed, the Harmonor who grants guidance even to the Masters. He would also redeem himself forever. He would—

"Good morning."

The voice startled Ned from his reverie. Looking up, he found a beautiful young woman standing before him in the street. He had almost run right into her, so distracted had he been while descending from the High Builder's workshop. "Dessina."

"Don't look so shocked," she told him. "Dismayed, even."

"Not dismayed, just—surprised. Delighted."

"Your face shows no delight."

"I just now finished meeting with the Lord High Builder," he said, "so my thoughts are in disarray."

"A good discussion, I hope?"

He nodded. "Yes, very good. But—complex."

"Have you met with any other Masters, too, in recent days?" she asked, looking mischievous.

Ned couldn't grasp what she meant. "Other Masters . . . ?"

Peeved now, Dessina said, "Must I mention what should be foremost in your thoughts? Or what I hoped would be? Which other Masters, you ask. The Master of Weddings, perhaps?"

He flustered. "Of course. Yes, the Master of Weddings. She's on my mind as well, given my upcoming appointment with her." Could Dessina detect his lie? She watched him as a cat watches a mouse just before pouncing.

"What a relief. I wouldn't have known, of course, except for your telling just now. I do hope you'll consider me worthy of hearing further news at a time you find convenient," she said. "Assuming, of course, that there's any news at all. Assuming, too, that you regard me as worthy of hearing such news."

"Trust me," Ned told her.

"I'm trying."

16

What, Allu asked herself, had taken place between her and Ned in that strange room full of instruments? Why had he suddenly told her to leave? She couldn't make sense of it. Had she made a mistake? If so, she couldn't imagine what the mistake might have been. It's true that she had sought Ned out: had walked up the steep streets and staircases to his studio. Having worked so hard to find him, she was responsible in this sense. Yet Ned himself had invited her inside. Had let her see his workshop. Had led her up to the storehouse. Had showed her all those instruments. Had demonstrated how some of them functioned, how they sounded. Had played that flute. Had, to her astonishment, joined her in a kind of conversation not by speaking but by playing and singing. Both Ned and Allu had clearly felt a mix of shock and delight to create music together. Then, abruptly, Ned had pulled away from her. Why? How could playing and singing have been a problem? Have been bad? She felt not only confusion but also annoyance, even anger, at his response. He had drawn back as if yanking his hand away from flames in a fireplace. This made no sense.

Very well, then, she told herself: be that way. Treat me like a flame that could burn you. Offended and dismayed, Allu put Ned out of her thoughts. She had plenty on her mind without wasting time on a silly boy.

For this reason she pursued her studies with great intensity. Allu sang with the Middle Choir, studied with the Middle Master, and learned everything she could about the powerful music of Sifirithi. She quickly discovered she could sing better than all the other students in the Middle Choir.

The quality of her singing, however, soon led to a surprise. The Middle Master took her aside one day and said, "My child, you cannot remain with us here."

"Haven't I done what you've told me?" she asked, feeling startled and upset. "Haven't I sung well?"

"You have done everything I've told you. You have sung very well indeed."

"So—why can't I stay?"

The Middle Master smiled. "Because you have sung too well. You have learned so quickly and so easily that I now have nothing more to teach you."

"I want to stay."

"My child, it's time for you to ascend once more. The High Master awaits you."

"Which High Master?"

"The only one—the Master of the High Choir."

Allu protested, but her words made no difference. Once again a servant arrived at her quarters, the old man urged her to be quick, Allu left with heim and they climbed the steep streets of Sifirithi all the way to the High Choir.

Allu shouldn't have worried. Once she reached the tower-like building that was the High Choir's home, the choristers present greeted her warmly. Only eight students made up the Choir; everyone else in the tower seemed to be servants. Allu was the youngest by far— many of the others were old men and women—and, as a result of her youth, she received almost constant attention and praise.

"Look at you!" exclaimed one of the other students, a bald man whose beard, reaching halfway down his chest, looked like a gray bib.

"Little more than a child!" As if in disbelief he reached out to touch Allu.

A white-haired woman said, "How well you must sing to have ascended at your age!"

"How lucky for Sifirithi!" said a wrinkle-faced man. "How lucky for Siir!"

The members of the High Choir made similar comments for a long time. Although shy at first, Allu enjoyed their attention. She was proud to be among them and felt happy to hear so much praise lavished on her.

She received more than just praise. Maids-in-waiting looked after Allu's every whim: a chair when weary, a meal when hungry, a bed when tired. Lords-in-waiting brought her meals so delicate that even the Middle Choir feasts now seemed like coarse Lowland food. Tailors visited Allu, measured her, and returned just a few hours later with finer garments than she had ever seen before. Allu dressed in them eagerly. *Bell-cloth.* Soft on the inside, her new robes had hundreds of tiny bells stitched to the outside—none bigger than thimbles, most far smaller—so that every step Allu took became music; every shiver and shake became music; every yawn, sigh, groan, giggle, and breath became music.

Yet none of this mattered much to Allu. She hadn't come here to wear fancy clothes. She had come here to sing. She had ascended from the Low Choir to the Middle, and from the Middle to the High, because of her singing. What mattered to Allu was singing. All she wanted was to keep singing.

That same afternoon Allu joined the other High Choir students for practice. A thin old woman attired in bellcloth bade her welcome. Tall and handsome, she was notable for the length of her pure white hair, which trailed all the way down her back like a waterfall.

"All in harmony."

"All in harmony."

"I am the High Master," she explained, "and my honor is to teach you now."

"It's my honor to be taught," Allu replied.

"You have met the others already?" She gestured at the elderly men and women who stood close by, all gazing at Allu.

"I have."

"Well, then," said the High Master, "you will now learn what all people would desire to know if they could ever imagine."

"I hope the songs are beautiful," Allu said.

Some of the High Choir students laughed gently at Allu's remark. The High Master laughed, too. "Beautiful? Beauty is the least of it."

The seven other singers now stepped forth and surrounded a small table now between themselves and the High Master. Allu took her place among them. When the Master snapped her fingers, a servant brought two straight-backed chairs and placed them near the table. The Master seated herself, then told Allu, "Please join me."

Though puzzled, Allu walked over and sat in the second chair.

Now the Master raised her right hand to signal the servants and stated: "Teapot, cups, and tea."

Allu wasn't sure what she meant.

One of the servants brought a small copper pot and set it on the table. Then he left briefly, returning with two pottery cups and a small wooden box.

"Would you like some tea?" the High Master asked Allu.

"If you please," Allu said reluctantly, though unsure why the Master would waste time serving tea during a lesson.

"Very well," the Master told the gathered choristers. "Let us sing what we sing." A stuttery, rough melody rose from the High Master's throat.

> Cold water, listen!
> You are no longer resting in a mountain lake!
> You are no longer streaming down a hillside!
> You must grow warm now! Grow warm!

Everyone in the choir imitated the Master.

After listening for a few moments, Allu impulsively reached toward the copper pot and cupped its sides with both hands. The metal was cold. "Where's the fire?" she asked, nodding toward the hearth across the room. This Master was so old that she couldn't even recall how to boil water!

The Master laughed gently. "In the High Choir we have no need of fire." Once again she sang her rough melody, and the Choir followed suit.

Allu held back her questions. Hesitating at first, she began to sing. Soon she had learned the new melody, its notes bubbling into the chill morning air.

Simply sitting there on the table, the pot looked exactly as before. Allu blurted out, "What good is it—"

"Here," said the Master. Her own hand guided Allu's until she touched the copper.

It was warm.

Once again they sang. Allu listened more closely to the Master, shaped the notes more carefully, brought them forth more clearly. The High Master glanced at her across the table and nodded.

> Warm water, listen!
> Do not stay idle now, as before!
> You must serve a worthwhile purpose!
> You must grow hot now! Grow hot!

When Allu looked into the pot, she saw tiny bubbles forming at the bottom. She sang louder.

Some of the bubbles grew, trembled, and rose toward the surface. She sang still louder.

The water in the pot started to simmer.

Allu sang even louder.

To her surprise, the water began to boil.

Though falling silent, the High Master motioned for the Choir to keep singing. She reached down to the wooden box, removed the lid, and grasped a bundle of the dark leaves nestled within. She sprinkled them into the pot. Hissing, the water engulfed the leaves. "Keep singing!" the Master told the Choir. As the choristers complied, she stirred the pot with a wooden spoon. Then, using her robe's heavy sleeves to protect her fingers from the hot metal, she grasped the pot's handles and poured some of the beverage into each of the two pottery cups. "Enough," she said.

The choristers fell silent.

Allu stopped singing too.

The High Master reached out with one of the cups.

She took it.

Using both hands, the Master raised her cup to eye level. "To the Harmonor," she said.

"To the Harmonor," said the Choir.

"To the Harmonor," Allu repeated.

They drank.

17

Ned began his experiments two days later. True to the Lord High Builder's promise, Ned acquired all materials he requested: wood of many varieties; metal of eight or ten different kinds; white bones of many sizes; glass crafted into tubes, bowls, and spheres; and various live animals, mostly birds but also three cats, a small dog, eight mice, a weasel, a rabbit, and two snakes, each beast housed in its own cage. Ned also received wooden boxes full of tools: saws, hammers, tongs, awls, and other implements. Assistants too: three lads and three lasses, each near his own age, each looking eager to help Ned in his quest to create new instruments. Gazing at this bounty—all these materials, tools, and young people now gathered in the huge new workshop that the High Builder had placed at his disposal—Ned felt pleased yet also alarmed. The weight of the Master's expectations burdened him. The sheer abundance so many supplies left him dizzy. The assistants' earnest expressions inspired alarm rather than confidence. "Thank you," Ned told them impulsively, "but I won't need your services. Not yet, anyway. Please return to your halls. I will contact you when I want your help."

Clearly disappointed, the six youths lingered briefly, then left.

Ned left, too, retreating at once to his own workshop.

≈ ≈ ≈

For one full day and part of the next he stood at his windows and gazed at the city below, he wandered through his workshop examining tools and materials, and at times he lay on his bed staring blankly at the ceiling. His mind roared with questions. Like a river in springtime, Ned's ideas first trickled, then flowed, then rushed like torrent filling the channel, then swelled to the point of nearly overflowing. Could he fashion a flute from condor bones? Could he make a bigger, louder flute out of a glass pipe? Could he even fashion a massive, powerful flute from hollow log? What about harps: was it possible to create one with more than a single set of strings? Two sets, even three? What about four sets, each forming the side of a box, so that the harpist stood inside the instrument to play? What of horns: was there a limit to their size? If the High Builder's goal was to create an instrument powerful enough to overwhelm opponents, why not create a horn big as a pine tree? Big as an oak, even, with six or eight people blowing into separate mouthpieces to combine their breath and thus power the instrument? Drums: was there any limit to how large and powerful they could be? Could Ned fashion a drum as big as a cow? Big as a haystack? Big as a barn?

These and a hundred other questions gushed through Ned's mind, pulling him into the roiling river of his thoughts, sweeping him downstream, buffeting him as he struggled to keep his head above the surface, leaving him exhausted until at last the river widened, the current slowed, and Ned somehow succeeded in crawling into a calmer state of mind somewhat like a beach. He lay there. He lost all awareness. He slept through the early morning hours, all of the next day, and halfway through the next night.

Then, with darkness once again cloaking Sifirithi below his windows, Ned forced himself out of bed, ate a quick meal, and set to work.

18

The High Master set a crystal goblet on a pedestal. Glinting in the torches' firelight, this was the finest glassware Allu had ever seen. "So beautiful!" she said quietly.

"I'm glad you like it," the Master responded. "Now shatter it."

Had she heard her right? "Shatter it?"

"Indeed."

Glancing at the lovely goblet—which, if sold, would have yielded enough money to feed her family for a year—Allu asked, "Why, Master? Why would I do that?"

"To prove your strength."

"It doesn't take much strength to shatter a glass." With those words she prepared to make her hand sweep the cup off its pedestal.

The Master reached out to allu and calmly restrained her. "Shatter it using only your voice."

She felt stunned. "My voice . . ."

"Some singers can wield their voices like a hammer," the Master told her. "No doubt you are one of them."

Allu stared at the goblet. She could think only of how much she wanted it—not for herself, but as a gift to bestow on her family.

"What are you waiting for?" asked the Master. "Sing."

"I don't want to break it."

"Breaking is the whole point."

"You won't be angry?"

"No—delighted."

"Even if I make a mess?"

"Make the biggest mess possible. Scatter bits of glass through the whole room, for all I care."

Without making a clear decision to proceed, Allu started to sing. Just one note: wide, heavy, and massive as a brick.

Nothing happened. The goblet rested there, still intact.

She tried again, louder now.

Once again she saw no change.

"Try something else," said the Master.

Allu sang a broad note, less a massive weight dropped on the glass than a blow struck from the side, much as her father sometimes chopped at a tree trunk with his axe.

Still no change.

"Sorry," Allu blurted, feeling embarrassed about her failure.

"There's no need to apologize," the Master stated gently. "Take your time."

Reassured, Allu relaxed, took a few steps toward the door, walked back, and scratched an itchy spot on her nose. Then she stood before the pedestal again, focused, and sang. This time the note resembled the hammers her parents used in their work as ironsmiths: small but strong, capable of directing concentrated force against heated metal to shape it. Allu sustained the note for a long time. Surely this would demolish the goblet!

The goblet stayed intact.

Allu stared in discouragement. Nothing she tried had even—

The cup suddenly cracked.

"Oh!" she cried out.

The goblet, now fractured from the lip all the way the bowl, didn't fall apart; it still rested upright on the pedestal. Yet the damage was obvious both to Allu and the Master.

They turned to each other and smiled.

"Well done," the Master stated plainly.

Allu felt excitement and pride to see her accomplishment. Then at once a shadow fell over these emotions. "That wasn't good enough," she said. "It's barely broken."

"True," the Master noted. "All the more reason to proceed."

Allu sang a note like a carving knife.

A note like a soup ladle.

Like a spatula.

Like a nutcracker.

Like an ice pick.

Like a sewing needle.

A web of cracks suddenly spread across the goblet, which collapsed at once, scattering splinters of glass across the top of the pedestal and onto the floor beneath it.

Stunned at first, Allu couldn't even react to what she'd done. Then she turned to the Master and, shyly, smiled.

The Master smiled. "I believe that would qualify as shattering."

Allu felt a surge of delight. This lesson was the best ever—a splendid way to conclude the day's work.

Before she could leave the room, however, the Master said, "That was a good start."

"Start?" Allu inquired. "We're not done yet?"

"Not quite."

"I shattered the glass."

"You did indeed."

"Isn't that enough?"

"It's enough for shattering," said the Master, "but other options need attention."

She gestured in puzzlement. "What options?"

The High Master beckoned to a servant. A man rushed over with a broom and a dustpan which, using quick motions, he used to remove the broken glass strewn across the floor and on the pedestal. The Master then directed the servant to bring a second goblet and place it where the first had rested. "Melt this one."

"*Melt* it!"

"Just like a glassblower melting a flawed goblet in the furnace."

Allu had seen a glassblower at work back in Laro, a woman whose boxlike furnace, glowing orange-yellow with fire inside and a little lake of molten glass pooling there, had both frightened and amazed her. "Like a flawed goblet in the furnace . . ." She sang a note that started out warm, grew hotter, and soon bathed the wine glass in something much like flames.

As with her efforts on the other goblet, nothing happened. The goblet rested on the pedestal; she saw no change. Disappointed, Allu reached out and, cautious as a cook, sensed its temperature by nearing but not touching the object with her hand.

Cold. Cold as the room itself.

She tried again, this time with a tighter note, a note that wasn't furnace-wide or furnace-deep but compact as a blob of hot glass clinging to a glassblower's blowpipe. Surely that note would melt a goblet!

It didn't. Reaching out again, however, Allu found the wineglass warm.

The Master smiled. She understood. Without bothering to test the goblet herself, he said, "Keep trying."

Perhaps a single note wouldn't be sufficient, Allu decided. Perhaps she needed something more substantial. Allu sang three notes, each acquiring heat from the previous, stoking some kind of fire that warmed crystal even if her flesh couldn't feel the heat.

Holding her hands near the goblet, she could sense its radiance.

"Don't stop," said the Master.

Allu didn't. She sang. She sang and sang. She sang until the glass began to glow—orange at the rim, dull red in the bowl itself. She sang until the entire goblet turned red-orange, then orange, then vivid orange-yellow. She sang until it softened and started to sink into itself. She sang until the bowl widened, slumped outward, and collapsed like an old mushroom on a rotting tree trunk.

Neither Allu nor the Master spoke at first. Then Allu, pleased with herself, asked, "Is that good enough?" The Master would now be satisfied, Allu thought—would let her finish up the day's lessons.

"Good enough," the Master replied. "Yes, very good indeed."

"Thank you, Master," Allu said, preparing to leave.

"Before you go, however, I have just one last request."

"Master?"

"It's all very well to shatter and melt glass goblets, but some tasks are even more challenging."

"What could be more challenging than to use the voice—"

"Certain materials resist even more than glass," the Master said, interrupting Allu. "Certain—substances. I won't waste our time explaining. It's better that you experience the situation yourself." With those words she clapped twice, beckoned to the servants, and, when the old man approached, told him: "Bring the volunteers."

Puzzled, Allu watched the servant leave, then return just a short while later with six other people. Three women and three men accompanied the old man. They were varied in age—two young, two in midlife, and two advanced in years—with a woman and a man present in each pair. Their plain wool robes suggested ordinary roles within Sifirithi. Each looked somewhat uncertain but not afraid. Stepping closer to the Master's table, they stood in a rough cluster. None of them spoke.

"Excellent," said the Master. Then to the six adults: "Thank you for joining us, and for helping. Your task is simple: just listen to a song."

Allu heard the Master's words but had no idea what they meant. How were these people helping? Whose song would they hear?

Now the High Choir Master turned to Allu herself. "It's clear to all of us—*us* meaning the various Masters—that you have a remarkable voice. Your voice is a great gift, a great honor. In addition, we are aware that you sometimes sing songs other than those we teach you."

"I'm sorry," Allu said, suddenly alarmed, well aware that her own songs caused concern, even anger, among the Masters of Sifirithi. "I can't help it. They just come to me."

"Apparently so."

"I try to stop them—"

"Hush, now. Let me finish."

Allu nodded.

The Master went on: "You sing those puzzling songs. There's no need for you to stop. You must, however, use them properly."

"Properly?"

"I've learned that you sang a song not long ago, a song with powerful effects on some children who heard it. Mind you, the people here know nothing of such songs. It's time now to let them hear one."

"More children, perhaps?" Allu asked.

"No—our six visitors."

"But they aren't children."

"Indeed they aren't," said the High Master. "All the same, they should hear you. Please sing a song like what you sang those children."

During this discussion, the three men and three women—the volunteers, as the Master had called them—stood patiently, watching and listening. No one showed any concern about the words that Allu and the Master had been speaking. They simply waited. Allu observed them closely. What was the point, she wondered, of singing these grownups a lullaby?

"Please proceed," the Master stated.

Without decided what to sing or when to start, just letting the song come to her, Allu began.

> The mole in his burrow,
> The fox in her den,
> The worm in the furrow,
> The eel in the fen—

Nothing happened. The volunteers stood there, watched Allu, and listened.

> These creatures are weary;
> They all want to sleep—
> Sleep, sleep, sleep!
> Sleep, sleep, *sleeeeeep!*

Did something change? Allu couldn't tell. Then—unless her eyes had fooled her—she saw two or three of these people starting to blink, some of them repeatedly. One of the men rubbed his eyes like a drowsy toddler.

> The goats in their paddock,
> The sheep in their pen,
> The bulls on the hillock,
> The deer in the glen—

The Master looked at Allu and smiled. She nodded—and, as Allu noticed with surprise, the Master stifled a yawn.

> Like them you are weary;
> You too want to sleep—
> Sleep, sleep, sleep!
> Sleep, sleep, *sleeeeeep!*

Astonished, Allu saw one of the women take a step backwards, walk toward the doorway, and sit abruptly near the wall. Another woman staggered sideways, knelt, and lowered herself to the floor. One of the men did the same.

> The stones in the quarry,
> The rain in the cloud,
> The words in the story,
> The corpse in the shroud—

The third woman turned, crouched, and sat, scarcely managing to ease her body down before collapsing. The other two men, grabbing at each other for support like shipwrecked sailors afloat in the sea, sank together and flopped over.

Allu couldn't believe what her eyes showed her.

"Don't stop," the Master said, bracing herself against the tabletop for support.

All six volunteers now lay curled or stretched out on the floor.

> Sleep, sleep, sleep!
> Sleep, sleep, *sleeeeeep!*

When she stopped singing, Allu heard the sound of slow, deep breathing. That, and the raspy noise of occasional snores.

"Was that the lullaby you wanted?" Allu asked, turning.

With her head now resting on the tabletop, the Master, too, was fast asleep.

19

ettling into the Lord High Builder's workshop, Ned said, "I'm ready to show you my first experiments."

"Excellent," the High Builder responded at once. "I'm sure you've devised some remarkable instruments."

"Quite a few."

"We may well need them."

"Master," Ned stated abruptly, "you told me the situation was urgent." The High Builder's sense of uncertainty—*We may well need them*—puzzled Ned. "The thieves and traitors down in the Lowland—we must restrain them."

The High Builder nodded. "Indeed we must. Rest easy: your instruments may provide the restraints. As it so happens, however, we have acquired something else, something powerful, for just that purpose."

"Some other instrument?" Ned felt his spirits sink. Who else in Sifirithi could have invented something, anything, better than Ned himself?

"One might say that, yes—though not an instrument made of wood, metal, or glass. Rather, of flesh and bone. A young lass— You see, there's a Newcomer with a remarkable voice. More so than any we've heard before."

Allu! Ned almost blurted her name out, then restrained himself. He asked, "Who is the lass?"

The High Builder waved the question away as if dispersing smoke. "Her name is of no consequence. The girl herself is unimpressive—at least until she sings. When she sings, however, calling her remarkable is too mild a word. She is . . . astonishing. I'll say no more. I'll say simply that she's what we need. What all of us need for the good of Sifirithi, the good of Siir."

"How so, Master?"

"To defend ourselves."

"Master—"

"Don't concern yourself too much with what's happening, Ned. We have the situation under control. Go back to your workshop. Resume your experiments. We will need your new inventions. You will accompany this young singer—accompany in several senses of the word. So: proceed."

Ned stayed in his chair beside the High Builder's table. He wanted to get up but couldn't. His efforts to imagine and design new instruments had come to a different outcome than he had expected. *You will accompany this young singer* . . . Allu—a Newcomer, a half-wild, untrained lass from the Lowland—had easily accomplished what Ned himself had struggled to achieve. Yet when he thought of Allu, he felt no anger. No jealousy. No contempt. Instead, he felt some kind of concern, even alarm, a feeling he couldn't identify. Would Allu's voice be the Masters' weapon against the Lowland rebels? If so, what did that mean for Allu herself? Other people could use Ned's instruments without him being present. He could build flutes, horns, drums, and whatever else he invented; then the Song Guards could transport the instruments down into the Lowland and deploy them against the rebels. But Allu: only Allu could sing with her own voice. *You will accompany this young singer* . . .

"I believe you should be going now."

Ned jolted out of his reverie. The Lord High Builder gestured toward the doorway.

"Sorry, Master," Ned stood and crossed the room.

"One last thing."

"Master?"

"Congratulations."

Unclear why the High Builder would congratulate him now after this difficult discussion, Ned asked, "For . . . ?"

"Your upcoming marriage."

Ned felt a chill spread through his flesh. "Master?"

The High Builder smiled. "Don't be so modest. Or secretive. I crossed paths with the Master of Weddings just this morning. She told me of your betrothal. Told me the date, even. That lovely Dessina—what a splendid wife she'll be."

VII

THE LULLABY WAR

20

Autumn ended and winter began. Winter in the Lowland had always been harsh—sleet, snow, and furious wind—but winter up high in Sifirithi was even worse. Snow fell day after day. Wind battered the towers. The cold intensified until Allu could feel it trying to nip her, bite her, and attempt to eat her alive. She never felt uncomfortable, however, because she could sing away even the worst weather. The snow never fell on her. The cold never seeped into her room. Even the wind didn't dare shriek at her window: Allu would simply sing it away. She went about her business ignoring the storms that raged all around.

Allu walked down into the city each winter day (a bubble of summer warmth surrounding her) and she saw that other people didn't fare so well. Their houses couldn't hold back the wind; they stumbled about in their huge coats. Allu almost felt sorry for them but withheld her pity. These people were all content, laughing and singing: even if winter chilled their flesh, it didn't freeze their good spirits. They looked happy. The chimes of Sifirithi made sure of it, all that music streaming down from the archways and balconies. And the chimes were only part of what cheered the city's inhabitants. Singers from the Middle Choir did, too. Groups of them sang in the streets, others in the Great Circle, still others on the surrounding towers' balconies. Music swirled through the air. Wandering, Allu expected all those melodies to combine in confusing, even repulsive ways, as unpleasant as too many kinds of food served at the same meal, but somehow they mixed together just right. Sifirithi was so festive that its people seemed on the verge of dancing in the streets.

✎ ✎ ✎

Later, when Allu had returned to her apartment, she heard a knock, opened the door, and found Sorrik standing on the other side.

"So what I hear is true," he said, stepping into the front room. "My dear friend has already ascended to the High Choir."

"You're back!" Allu exclaimed, embracing the old emissary. "I thought I'd never see you again! Please come in. I've missed you. Where have you been?"

"I had to leave for a while," he said. "I would have visited you sooner, but you move about so fast you're difficult to find."

"The High Master wanted me here."

"So I see."

Allu whirled about, letting her bell cloth robe jingle. "Isn't it wonderful? Bell cloth! What could be better than bell cloth?"

"You have done well." Smiling, Sorrik gazed at her.

"The High Master is so pleased that she'll teach me everything."

Sorrik nodded. "Everything she knows."

"Everything! I want to know everything!"

Sorrik's expression now grew serious. "The Master of the High Choir is the finest of all the singing Masters," he said, "but she herself would admit to certain kinds of ignorance."

"She's the High Master."

"True, but still ignorant."

Allu started feeling restless. The old man wasn't making sense. She told him, "I'll study with someone else, then—whoever knows what the High Master doesn't."

"Be careful," Sorrik said quietly. "Some things only one person knows."

"Only one person? Which person?"

"Who else but the Harmonor."

Allu wasn't impressed. "Fine. I'll learn what the Harmonor knows."

The emissary took Allu gently by the arm. "You mustn't speak so carelessly."

"I don't understand," she told Sorrik. "Who is the Harmonor, anyway? Why can't I learn what the Harmonor—"

"I urge you not to ask what you cannot understand. Even the Masters ask no questions about the Harmonor. A mere child—"

"I'm not a child. I'm sixteen—and the High Master calls me her best student."

"Even the best cannot understand some things."

"How can I understand what no one will explain?"

"Through silence," Sorrik told her.

"Silence?"

"Let me warn you," he went on, his forehead creased. "You will understand only by silence."

Suddenly afraid—Allu had never seen her old friend looking so tense—she said, "I never wanted to say anything—"

"Then say *nothing.* You cannot imagine how far even a small voice carries. Will you go on? Will you ask yet more questions?" Sorrik clutched the sides of his head with both hands. "Allu, Allu, forgive me! You understand so much, yet so little! Be careful, please! Enough of your questions!"

21

Dessina, Ned told himself. An image bloomed in his mind. Her lovely face, her impressive cape of black hair, her steady-staring blue eyes . . . This image didn't delight him, however; it frightened him. To marry Dessina! How like Dessina to arrange their wedding on her own, as if Ned were just a passenger along for the ride! A ride he didn't want to take. How could he stop this voyage before it started?

Another image came to him now: the face wind-weathered, the eyes brown, the hair short and messy, the mouth smiling in amusement or mockery. Allu, the strange Lowlander . . . Why was she here in Sifirithi, and what should Ned do about *her?* Pay her no mind? Willfully avoid her? She was nothing but trouble. Yet while staring at this apparition, Ned felt less concern about himself than about her. Concern—and some kind of longing he couldn't identify. Did Allu have any notion of what the Masters were planning? Of what they intended as her role in the plan? If so, was participation her own decision? Or was she just drifting along, carried away like a wind-blown leaf?

22

Look at the tree outside my window," the High Master told Allu. She gestured with her twig-like fingers. "The year is almost done. The leaves have withered. Bring them back, my child. Bring back their green, summery luster. The fruit, too: bring back the fruit."

Although hesitant, Allu obeyed these orders. She sang the Anthem to Reverse the Seasons—quietly at first, then louder—and observed the tree for changes. Allu felt disappointed, for nothing happened. When she held back for a moment, however, the High Master joined in abruptly, motioning for Allu to continue. Allu resumed singing. A minute or two passed. She grew impatient. Then, without noticing the exact moment, Allu saw how the dull, curled leaves scarcely clinging to the branches now turned glossy. Brown transformed itself into green. The wrinkled, rust-colored apples dangling there swelled and turned bright red, bending the limbs.

Allu fell silent.

"Keep singing!" the Master commanded.

Allu started up once again. The apples now faded from red to green, shrank, then disappeared altogether. A moment later, blossoms sprang up in their place.

The High Master said, "Enough!" and raised a hand to silence Allu. "Now sing the Anthem to Advance the Seasons." Allu did as the Master told her. The flowers diminished and disappeared; the apples appeared again, puffed up, greened, reddened, wrinkled once more, and dropped off the tree; the leaves darkened, fluttering to the ground.

By means of these anthems Allu learned how to sing plants out of the earth, though it was winter instead of spring. She learned how to sing flowers open, then sing them shut again. She learned how to sing bees out of their hive, butterflies out of their cocoons, and birds out of their nests. Not only that: she learned how to sing hot weather into cold and cold weather into hot. She learned how to sing dusk into midafternoon and sunrise into the darkest night. She learned how to sing sunshine out of the clouds and rain out of a clear sky.

All it took was the right anthem.

Learning the High Master's lessons, Allu delighted in her new knowledge and in the power it granted her. Soon she could now do easily what had been difficult, even impossible, before. She could freshen stale food. She could sweeten sour milk. She could brighten a shadow-filled room. She could warm a cold bed. Allu couldn't imagine ever being hungry, thirsty, cold, or uncomfortable ever again. The anthems worked well, each in its own way. A separate anthem existed for every purpose. Singing the anthems, Allu now felt less at the mercy of her surroundings. This was surely as it ought to be. The High Choir anthems served the right purpose for those few persons allowed to use them. Allu had gained access to the High Choir anthems, so she could sing them now for her own benefit. Wasn't that enough?

At times, however, feeling dazed, Allu withdrew into bewilderment and longing. She couldn't make sense of how much had happened since she left Laro not long ago. She was only a villager, she told herself. She felt confused by this city, its people, and their ways. Even thinking of Laro made her dizzy. Her parents, her sisters, her brother—what were they doing now? Eating supper beside the hearth? Settling in for a cold night? Telling tales before bedtime—or perhaps wondering about Allu and what she was doing? Allu missed them. She felt a great pang of pity for the hard life they lived. She wished she could speak with them, ask how they were, and reassure them about her own circumstances.

At the same time, she felt a twinge of annoyance, even contempt, toward her family. To think that they huddled together, incapable of sparing themselves their wintry discomfort! Even a few phrases of an anthem would have eased the chill. How could she muster sympathy for people so helpless to ease their woes?

Surely, Allu told herself, the few people possessing the High Choir knowledge deserved to know what they knew. She should feel no shame in benefiting from the notes she sang, which, like seeds cast onto fertile ground, had sprouted, grown, blossomed, and borne fruit. These anthems were Allu's share of the harvest. She shouldn't feel ashamed to enjoy the feast now set before her. It was good and proper to learn what the High Master taught. It was enough to serve Sifirithi by singing.

Just one thing puzzled her. Allu couldn't bring back the voices that had come to her in the past. She spent many hours in her room alone. She waited. She even sang to them hoping that whoever had sung back so often would sing once again. The High Master sometimes asked why she chose to be alone upstairs instead of joining the other choristers in the common rooms below. She answered that the lessons exhausted her; she needed to rest. Though puzzled, High Master accepted this explanation. So too did the choristers, for they themselves knew that their studies were strenuous, and surely even more so for someone so young. Allu stayed in her room with the door closed and bolted.

She sat there and waited.

No voices came to her.

Allu missed them. She wondered why they had fallen silent. She tried beckoning to them, though unsure how. Should she call out? Sing first? Simply wait?

Nothing made a difference. The dreamsongs stayed away.

Sitting by the window, she looked out and saw everything below her—the city aglow with torchlight; the cliffs dropping away on each side; the valleys brimming with shadow—and she felt as if this whole place belonged to her. Sifirithi spread out like a servant bowing at her feet. She could bring down sleet on its houses, or bright sunshine. She could silence the chimes by holding the wind back, or else stir up gusts and make loud music. She could do almost anything she wanted. Looking out from the highest room in the highest tower on that mountaintop, Allu could have sung the people of Sifirithi into doing whatever she wanted them to do.

Then she looked out again, this time across the empty air between the near summit and the far one. Dusk was falling. The city shimmered below. Some of the lights extended up the lower reaches of the other mountain. Unlike the peak that Allu had gradually ascended during her studies, however, that far one was mostly dark. Halfway up its steep sides, all lights ended. Except for the top: and there, like the first star that night, shone the light from a single dwelling.

Allu sat, gazing outward and upward, for a long time. What sort of dwelling, she wondered, would cast such a light? And what sort of person would live there?

23

"Why have you come here?" Allu asked him when Ned arrived at her room in the High Tower.

"To explain," he replied quietly, since he was still standing in the hallway and didn't want to risk being overheard.

"Explain what?"

He faltered. Only then did he realize how vague his concerns must have sounded, no doubt too vague to explain.

"Go on," she told him. Standing in the open doorway, Allu didn't let him enter.

"May I speak with you in private?" Ned asked.

"In the common hall downstairs."

"That's not so private."

His voice must have been convincing, however, since Allu stepped aside, allowed him into the room, and closed the door.

Ned found her quarters startling: even more splendid than he had expected, vast and elegant, with well-crafted furniture throughout the room and fine tapestries on the walls. What impressed him most of all were the tall windows gazing out over the city. "Quite a panorama."

"Have you come here," she asked, "just to admire the view?"

"Of course not."

"You promised me an explanation."

"I did. There have been—developments."

As if ignoring him, she walked over to the windows and gazed outward. "What might those be?"

Ned followed her. "They are difficult to explain. The Masters have made some decisions."

"That's what the Masters do, isn't it? That's why I trust them—they decide what's best for us. All of us. I feel safe in their hands."

"Even if those hands act rashly?"

"Not rashly—wisely."

"Even if those hands move you like a pawn in a game?"

"I trust the game they're playing."

Ned felt thwarted, outfoxed. How could he explain what he himself couldn't fully grasp? All he understood was his concern toward this strange, half-wild creature standing before him. "Sing for me." His voice startled Ned himself as well as Allu.

"Sing," she echoed, examining the word like an odd, shiny stone. "Which anthem?"

"No anthem. Just what you sing—your own songs."

"My songs serve no purpose."

"Sing anyway."

"Why bother if they serve no purpose?"

"Just sing for me. *To* me."

Allu stared at him for a long moment.

He had offended her, Ned now saw, had even angered her. He expected her to change the subject. But then she sang.

> I am here, you are there, and now we stand,
> Not knowing what we think at all.
> What to say? What to do? We still don't know.
> Yet we watch, yet we wait, yet we stall.

Singing this melody and its words, Allu looked uneasy, even shocked, as if she herself found the song unfamiliar. Ned listened. He delighted in her singing. A shiver ran up his spine. His shoulders gave a quick shudder. Ned had rarely sung before—he couldn't, he shouldn't—yet now he, too, sang.

You are there, I am here, and now we stand,
Not knowing what we think at all.
Who are you? Who am I? We still don't know.
Yet we watch, yet we wait, yet we fall.

Like two seeds that sprout in the soil, push upward, unfold their leaves, and reach toward the light, their melodies grew like tendrils bumping into each other and intertwining until they became a single plant.

We are here, we are here, and now we stand,
Not knowing what to understand—

"What are we to do?" she asked.
"I don't know yet."
"Nor do I."

24

Allu felt surprised when, just a day later, the High Master took her aside. "There is some trouble, my child, and you must help us."

"Trouble?" Allu asked. "What kind of trouble?"

"In the Lowland. Come, we need your help." The Master led Allu toward some servants who awaited them in the hallway.

Allu pulled back. "I don't understand," she said. "How will I be helping? Can't you explain?"

The Master said, "You will assist the Song Guards." Before Allu could ask about the Song Guards, the Master continued: "They are members of the Middle Choir who serve as the guardians of Siir—an army of singers far more powerful than mere soldiers. When fools and traitors threaten the realm, the Song Guards go forth to protect everyone from foolishness and treason."

"By singing the right anthem."

"Exactly: the right anthem. If a thief steals bread, the Song Guards sing the Anthem to Catch Thieves. If a merchant cheats his customers, the Song Guards sing the Anthem to Inspire Honesty. If a peasant—"

"I'm no longer part of the Middle Choir," she reminded the High Master.

The old woman nodded. "Of course. You are no ordinary Song Guard. Believe me, this trouble is no ordinary trouble—"

Frightened but eager, Allu told her, "I'll help in whatever way I can."

"You must," he said. "Sifirithi depends upon you."

25

"W e need your assistance," the Lord High Builder told Ned that same day.

"Master?"

"Gather up your new instruments—the drum, the horn, and all the rest. The Song Guards will arrive at your workshop along with a team of carriers to transport them."

"Transport them where?" Ned asked. He felt both curious and alarmed. What might be happening that would require the use of his untested inventions?

The High Builder said, "The runners will transport them to where you, too, will be going."

"I?"

"Who else?" The High Builder added, "Prepare yourself for a brief trip to the Lowland."

26

Allu and Ned left the city one day later. Along with two Song Guard captains, they departed in a sleigh pulled by eight strong runners. Twelve other sleighs, each transporting other Song Guards and loads of equipment, left with them. This caravan wound its way down from the mountains into the Lowland. Snowfall made the rough travel still rougher, the long journey even longer.

Inside the sleigh's compartment, Allu sat with Ned on a padded bench while the captains—a man and a woman—sat opposite. Both looked pale and cold in their ornately embroidered woolen gowns. The compartment felt cozy but cramped. The journey itself confused her: she had no idea where they might be, even less where they were going. When she peered out the window, Allu saw nothing but grainy whiteness. The two Song Guard captains amused each other by singing—first the Anthem to Raise Low Spirits, then the Anthem to Ease Weariness. Allu listened and at times joined in. She considered singing some of the High Choir anthems (the Anthem to Hasten Slow Voyages, perhaps) but held off. She felt tired. Allu didn't feel like singing, only resting. She glanced sideways at Ned; he glanced back; they said nothing. The rocking of the sleigh soon put her to sleep.

She woke with a start. She heard no sound from the runners, the coachman, the Song Guards, or Ned, but she saw that her companions had already woken. The captains looked outside. Moving slowly, the sleigh passed among fog-shrouded shapes. Allu couldn't make sense of her surroundings. What would happen now? She felt uneasy but eager to do whatever the captains might ask of her. She would collaborate with Ned, too, if he wanted. She would sing, ward off trouble, and help restore harmony.

Then, gazing out through the snowfall, she saw the blurry features of a town: cottages and shops. No people. No cobblers, blacksmiths, butchers, bakers. No shopkeepers or children. "What is this place?" Allu asked. "Where is everyone?"

One of the captains, a big bald man, replied, "Hiding. A band of traitors is active here, so the townspeople have fled."

"What traitors?"

"Who knows!" said the other captain, a pale woman. "All traitors are the same. They are *traitorous*. We must defeat them."

The sleigh proceeded, now more slowly. Allu could see a few houses: thatched roofs, windows, doorways . . . The sleigh stopped. Allu felt a twinge of alarm. This place frightened her. Who were the traitors? What treason had they committed? Their deeds must surely be harmful and dangerous. Then, looking at the captains, she felt a surge of confidence and pride. She would do her part—anything they asked of her—to rid this town of traitors.

One of the captains spoke to the coachman through a little hatch: "Well? What is it?"

"Our own forces," came the reply. "Song Guards are beckoning. You should go forth on foot."

The captains spoke to each other in low voices. Allu, listening, couldn't make sense of their words.

"—following our instructions," the woman said.

"—not much choice," the man said.

Allu looked at Ned to guess what he might be thinking. He nodded, smiled faintly, but said nothing.

After the captains conferred a while longer, the woman turned to Allu and Ned: "You should mobilize to do what you've come here for."

The captains buttoned up their coats, pulled on fur gloves and caps, and prepared to leave the sleigh. "Get ready," one of the men told Allu and Ned.

Allu felt afraid again, but only for a moment, as she hummed the Anthem Against Fear to calm herself. By then Ned and the captains had opened the door and stepped out. Allu saw no alternative but to follow.

"Hurry!" someone cried out in the dim light.

Allu ran after the others. Snow and fog surrounded her. Slipping about on the icy road, she nearly fell, regained her footing, then rushed on. A few moments later she arrived at a barricade where a small troop of Song Guards, fifteen or twenty of them, had taken cover. Their gray, scarlet, and yellow-orange robes marked them as members of the Middle Choir. Each wore a copper helmet plumed with a scarlet feather.

Allu couldn't see much at first; then her eyes adjusted. Little by little she made sense of her surroundings. She could see several badly damaged houses and shops right across the road: windows broken, shutters torn off, doors ripped away, roof-tiles scattered. Stones and pieces of wood lay in the snowy street. Allu, growing angry, asked, "The traitors did this?"

One of the Song Guards—a colonel, perhaps, for he wore a bigger plume on his helmet—said, "Indeed."

"Who are they?"

"Traitors!" exclaimed the colonel. "A whole mob of them, every last one a traitor!"

Before Allu could speak again, the Song Guard captains asked the colonel, "Why haven't you captured them yet?" and "How many are inside?"

"The traitors are of uncertain number," replied the colonel. "They have taken some villagers hostage, however, so many people are trapped inside these houses. We hope to spare the innocent, if possible."

Allu listened, more and more confused. The situation here was even stranger than she had expected.

The male captain said, "Tell us who they are, then, so we can sing them into submission."

The female captain asked, "Are they thieves? Kidnappers? Killers? Knowing will help us determine the right anthem to use against them."

The plumed colonel shook his fist at the house. "Who knows what treason they commit!" he cried. "Anything! Everything! Deeds so foul I dare not describe them. Theft! Perfidy! Disobedience! Insults to the

Harmonor, even. Need I say more?" Then he added, "Do whatever you must, but do so quickly. How much time must we waste in this worthless place? If the traitors won't surrender, we'll burn the whole village."

Almost at once Allu heard the sound of weeping. She looked ahead and saw people in several houses peering out through some windows. Most of them pulled back at once; only a few kept watching. She couldn't see well in the dim light, but even a glimpse troubled her. Traitors? Hostages? She didn't know what to think. This colonel seemed harsh—why burn the whole town?—yet Allu feared the traitors as much as the Song Guards did.

She turned suddenly. Where was Ned? Tingling with alarm, Allu realized that he no longer stood beside her. "Ned?" she called out, her voice wavering.

At this same moment she noticed him, along with some of the Song Guards, about a dozen yards away, all of them pulling a sleigh. On the sleigh was a bizarre device. It resembled a huge wheel: tall as man, wider than Allu's arms could have reached from left to right, and pale in color. Allu thought at once of the great wheels of cheese that dairy farmers make back in Laro. Cheese! No, this object wasn't cheese. She called out to Ned: "What is it?"

Startled, he clearly heard Allu's voice but couldn't find its source. Then, catching sight of her, he called back: "A drum!"

"What's a drum?"

"You'll see," he answered. "Or rather—you'll hear."

As this exchnge took place, a small choir of Song Guards—seven or eight young women and men—lined up in two rows near the drum. At once they began singing.

> The drummer drums on his great big drum,
> And he'll drum and he'll drum till your head goes numb—
> And he'll drum and he'll drum till your mind goes dumb—
> Then he'll drum and he'll drum till you all succumb!

Calling out toward the village, the colonel now shouted out a threat: "Surrender, all of you! Surrender—or this weapon will destroy you!"

Allu heard no response. She could see a few faces peer out of the house, but no one answered or emerged.

"Proceed," Ned told one of the Song Guards.

A young man standing nearby nodded, picked up a long stick, heavy as a club, and began beating the drum.

Allu couldn't believe the noise. Like thunder rolling forth from a storm cloud, the sound burst out and smashed into everything around it. She could barely stay on her feet. Even Ned staggered back from the force. Allu cupped her hands to protect her ears.

The drummer kept drumming. The Song Guards backed off, clearly frightened. Even the falling snow parted as the vast noise pushed through it. On all the houses the windows rattled, the doors clattered, and many of the glass panes cracked or shattered.

Ned signaled for the drummer to stop.

When the young man ceased drumming, the colonel called out to the villagers: "Surrender—or else the drummer will resume!"

Silence fell over the village for a long moment.

A strange sound emerged from the traitors' house. Everyone listened for a moment. Then Allu heard the melody and the words:

> Like songbirds captive in a cage,
> We have too long been calm and still!
> Now let us risk the Masters' rage
> And sing a song to flex our will!

At once the Song Guards started singing the Anthem Against Evil. The tune took Allu by surprise. She forced herself to pay attention, took a deep breath, and joined in. The Guards' voices rose like startled pigeons. Allu couldn't help but smile to herself: so much for those traitors!

> Listen, you who cause great evil:
> We will crush you like a weevil!

The Song Guards sang loudly, then fell silent. Allu, Ned, and everyone else now waited.

The only response from inside the house was more singing.

> You threaten us with drums and fire,
> You take away our every choice,
> You batter us with hate and ire,
> Yet threats will never still our voice.

The Song Guards resumed singing, this time the Anthem to Suppress Anger. Allu sang with them. The gentleness of its melody, as warm as sunrise on a summer day, calmed her at once. This, if anything, would silence the traitors, would bring them forth. Who could resist the Anthem to Suppress Anger?

> Woe to you who rant and rave!
> Snuff this anger—and behave!

The anthem ended; silence hung in the air like snow. The traitors' house stood motionless and quiet. The Song Guards glanced at each other and smiled.

Then the traitors' song came forth again:

> The seasons wither; clouds are palling—
> Snow itself comes down alarmed.
> But even snowflakes tire of falling.
> The clouds disperse, the sky has warmed.

Allu was surprised to see that Ned, listening to the villagers, now turned abruptly and left. Several of the Song Guards followed him. She wondered for a moment if she too should leave. Was Ned abandoning his post? Shirking his duty? She couldn't imagine he would stop resisting the traitors. Then, just a short while later, she saw Ned return with a cluster of Song Guards, all of them pulling another sleigh through the snowfall. This sleigh, like the first, carried a strange device. Allu couldn't even guess what it was. Made of bright copper, it looked like a long hollow log, thick as a grown man's chest, but flared at one end. Five branch-like tubes extended sideways from the wide shaft. Much as soldiers might roll out a huge cannon—all the troops grunting and groaning as they pulled the weapon into place—so now did the Song Guards bring forth this massive device.

Allu kept her distance. She knew that this object was another of Ned's instruments. She couldn't even guess what it might do. Having heard the drum, however, she felt afraid. She watched as Ned and the Song Guards aimed the wide end of the metal device at the houses. Five members of the Guard took their positions near the branch-like tubes on both sides. She tensed up as Ned's helpers put their lips against the ends of the tubes and started blowing.

The noise blasted forth even louder than the drum's. Like the moans of a hundred dying animals—a herd of elk or moose—this appalling sound mixed with commotion like the crunch of boulders crashing through a steep forest. Hearing this awful racket, the gathered Song Guards backed off even as it started. All who lingered now cupped both hands against their ears. Allu did so as well. The great horn's death-moan smashed into everything and everyone.

Allu crouched, confused, unsure what was happening. The noise baffled her. She could see people shouting all around her but couldn't grasp the words. Between blasts of the terrible horn she heard screams and wails. She looked up, shielding her face with her hands, as if waiting to be struck, and at that moment saw such a terrible sight that she couldn't even cry out in dismay. The few unbroken windows on the house across the street cracked and shattered, the roof sagged, the walls bulged outwards. Allu, frozen in her own fear and curiosity, stood there watching. The house slumped onto itself like a rotten pumpkin. Dust billowed into the snowfall and obscured everything on that side of the street.

At first no one moved. Allu heard coughs and groans from the wreckage of the traitors' hiding place. As the dry cloud settled, however, two men emerged, both drenched in dust. Were they attacking? Allu stepped back, ready to run. But the men, ghostlike in their powdery shrouds, simply stood there. Then more people staggered out of the rubble. Men and women: six of them . . . eight or nine . . . a dozen . . . then twenty or more, all gray with dust. They looked about, coughing, rubbing their eyes, uncertain and wary. No one spoke.

Allu wished she knew another anthem, one powerful enough to dissolve these traitors into sand just as Ned's horn had dissolved their houses. What right did they have to sing? They scarcely deserved to live. Allu restrained herself. How pointless to waste even a single note on such pathetic people!

Traitors kept pouring out of the rubble: three dozen now, maybe more. Allu watched in astonishment. She hadn't imagined so many traitors in all of Siir. Yet their appearance baffled her: she could tell from their clothing—tattered wool, dirty cotton, greasy leather—that they were just villagers, farmers, tradespeople. She saw men and women and, to her surprise, children as well. Allu watched their silent surrender.

Then, last of all, a young woman walked out of the debris. Fifteen years old, maybe sixteen . . .

Allu stared at her, full of anger. To think that even this lass had joined the traitors! At least she, too, now had the sense to surrender.

Soon enough she reached an appalling insight: these people weren't surrendering. On the contrary, they now gathered together, grouped themselves like soldiers in a squadron, and prepared to fight. To fight by . . . singing.

Their voices rose at once and reached Allu, Ned, and the Song Guards through the snowfall.

> Like seeds in springtime, we will grow
> Despite our long sleep in the earth,
> And we will flourish row by row—
> A garden green with lush rebirth.

27

Watching the traitors as they gathered in the street, Ned knew he had failed. His drum had damaged the traitors' village, true enough, and the great horn had destroyed their hiding place. Even so, the instruments had failed. At least three dozen traitors now faced the Song Guards and sang fearlessly. Worst of all, they sang a song so defiant that even the Song Guard anthems couldn't dislodge the treason in the traitors' hearts.

Ned, Allu, and the Song Guards listened to these strange, filthy people as they massed before them and sang. The colonel and the captains glanced at one another. Members of the Song Guards, too, looked around as if awaiting commands from the officers.

The traitors kept singing.

> Then coming forth from our rich bounty . . .

At that moment something took place that Ned could never have predicted. It wasn't just that Allu herself started singing, for she had come here to sing. Rather, it was what and how she sang. Her song started slowly, calmly. Unlike the Song Guards' anthems, the melody was gentle, not harsh; the words soft, not hard.

> Hush, my darlings, to go sleep—
> Wade into the pool so deep.

Hearing this song, the traitors took notice but made no other response. They appeared to be listening. Some of them looked at their fellows as if asking a silent question. Others simply stared at Allu.

She continued to sing.

> Hush, O sweet ones, time to swim—
> The wind subsides, the light grows dim.

Most remarkable was a change that Ned saw but couldn't describe: something in the traitors' stance, their posture. They seemed—calm. Nothing in their expressions showed anger now. Nor tension. Nor resistance. They simply stood there, listening and waiting. A few even smiled.

Allu kept singing.

> Dive into that gentle lake—
> Go to sleep until you wake.

He realized at some point that not just the traitors, but Ned himself, felt unsteady. Some of the traitors took a few steps forward or to one side. Some backed away from the group. Ned, feeling dizzy, reached over to the sleigh on his right for support. He tried hard to stifle yawn. An astonishing sight reached his eyes: several traitors grabbed one another to avoid falling, others lowered themselves to the snowy ground, still others collapsed altogether.

The melody of Allu's song wafted and spread like snowfall. It dispersed everywhere. No one could avoid it. All of the people here felt it seep into their flesh and bones. Ned felt it weigh him down, too, weigh so heavily that he could no longer stay upright.

Before hitting the ground, he just barely managed to crouch, reach out with both hands, and break his fall.

28

The next day, following a long voyage back to Sifirithi, Allu saw people coming out to welcome the procession of sleighs. Hundreds waited by the roadside. Hundreds more cheered from windows and balconies when the sleighs passed through their towns.

"Long live Allu!" they cried.

"Long live Ned Jerosso!"

"Long live the Song Guards!"

The cheering lasted all the way into the city, where even larger crowds called out an even greater welcome. Hundreds of women, men, and children massed around the sleighs as the runners pulled them through the gates—so many people that when Allu emerged at last, she could scarcely work her way out of the city's center and climb the alleyways and staircases back to the High Tower.

"I have known all along that you can do anything with your voice," the High Master said, "but you have surprised me anyway. You deserve the highest praise we can offer. I am well pleased. The Harmonor, too, is pleased."

"I want only to serve the Masters and the Harmonor," Allu told him. She felt pride and relief warm her body. The traitors had been caught; Siir was now safe. All the better that Allu and Ned—Allu above all—had ended the traitors' rebellion.

No one let her forget: during the next few hours, she received a long series of visits—from the Masters, from their students, from the people of Sifirithi—each person offering Allu thanks, honor, and praise.

"Down with the enemies of Siir!" everyone cried out. "Long live Allu!"

The last person to visit was Sorrik. Allu almost didn't notice him at first, for the old emissary just stood in the doorway, hesitant.

She walked over to greet him. "Sorrik," she said. "How good of you to come."

Sorrik hugged her but lingered in the doorway.

Neither of them spoke. After a long silence, Sorrik said, "I would have come sooner, but it seemed best to wait."

"You are always welcome here." She gestured for him to enter.

Obeying her, Sorrik walked into the room, stepped over to a chair, and eased his body into it.

Allu sat next to him.

With his hands resting in his lap like weary birds, the old man stayed silent for a while, then asked, "Are you pleased?"

The question surprised her. "Of course," she told him, "We caught the traitors."

"So I've heard."

"No one got hurt. I put them to asleep—and then the Song Guards found it easy to capture them."

"I heard that as well."

"My lullaby made that possible."

"Indeed."

"It worked even better than I'd expected."

"You must be proud," said Sorrik.

Allu nodded but held back from speaking. Sorrik's hesitance puzzled her. "Are you feeling unwell?" she asked him.

"Not in the usual sense," he replied.

"In what sense, then?"

"Allu, I need to explain something—"

"If you are well," she told him, "let's talk tomorrow. We're both tired, aren't we?"

"Quite so." He gazed at her, somehow disappointed.

"Good," Allu said, growing wearing of the old man's strange mood. "You should go rest."

"Perhaps I should." With those words he stood carefully, crossed the room, and left.

29

Ned felt dizzy with confusion. The expedition to the Lowland had succeeded. Working together, Allu and Ned and the Song Guards had subdued the traitors. The Song Guards had set the stage by organizing the journey and providing logistical support. Ned's instruments had routed the traitors and destroyed their hiding places. Then Allu's lullabies had stunned the traitors into submission—had left them not only helpless but sunk in deep slumber. With this outcome, the Song Guards had made quick work of binding the unconscious traitors' hands and feet, loading them onto sleighs, and transporting them back to Sifirithi. The entire traitorous lot of them would sleep until they woke . . . and would find themselves trapped in a dungeon.

In short, the expedition was a great success.

Or was it?

Pondering the situation, Ned felt uneasy, not confident. Restless, not at peace. Worried, not pleased. Uneasy, not proud.

Were these misgivings a result of his instruments having proved less effective than Allu's lullabies?

No, something else nagged at him, as painful as foul food festering in his stomach.

30

Allu didn't know what to think of her odd conversation with Sorrik. He seemed so weary, so tense. Was he ill? Or maybe just tired? Perhaps the past few days' commotion—the crowds and the celebrations—had left him exhausted. Not surprising, she decided: he was so old. She decided not to worry.

Rather than concern herself with Sorrik, she chose to seek out Ned. She left the High Choir tower, descended the staircases and alleyways into the lower regions of Sifirithi, and walked to the Great Circle. Crowds still congregated there—so many people talking, laughing, and celebrating. Allu wandered among them and joined in the merrymaking. Some of the revelers noticed her presence and called out: "All in harmony! Long live Allu!" She called back, "All in harmony," chatted with some of her old friends or with strangers, and, when circumstances allowed, she broke away and kept searching for Ned. Perhaps he had retreated to his workshop?

She found him near the edge of the Circle. Alone. So much the better. Approaching, she felt surprised that he seemed not to notice her; or, if he noticed, that he didn't react. He showed neither surprise nor delight to see her.

"Hello."

"Hello." He smiled a weak smile.

"We did it."

"We did indeed."

Perplexed by his flat tone, Allu decided to cheer him with praise. "You were splendid. Your instruments were—"

"—weapons."

"Excuse me?"

"Just what I said. My instruments were weapons."

"A good thing, too," she told Ned. "Otherwise who knows what the traitors would have done? Your instruments damaged their hiding place and forced them out."

His expression startled and puzzled her: uneasy. "Music should give pleasure and offer solace, not cause pain and fear."

"But the traitors—"

"Did you see them?" he asked abruptly.

"Of course."

"You saw what terrible people they are?"

"That was obvious."

Ned gazed at her with unwavering eyes. "Tell me what you saw."

Allu hesitated. "Men and women," she told him. "Children too."

"And?"

"And what?"

"Were they armed? Were they wielding swords and lances?"

"Not that I could tell."

"Were they ready for battle?"

"They sang," Allu said firmly. "They wielded *songs*. All singing is forbidden, yet they *sang.*"

"That is their treason?"

"Part of it. Resisting the Song Guards too. Refusing to pay tribute. Who knows what else?"

"For these crimes," Ned told her, "we destroyed their homes and threatened to burn the entire town."

Annoyance boiled up inside her. "But we didn't hurt anyone!" she shouted. "We spared them! Nobody got hurt or killed!"

"Just put to sleep."

Now she couldn't restrain herself. "How was that a problem? Was it worse than attacking them with swords and fire? Are my lullabies, too, a weapon?"

"More like a poison," Ned said. "Or a potion—a sleeping potion. You dosed them with your potion and left them all as calm as babies in a crib."

"Lucky for them," Allu replied. "Let them sleep like babies. Let them awake refreshed, ready to face the new day, and willing to behave themselves."

"I hope your lullabies prove so healthful."

"I'm sure they will. A good sleep would benefit everyone."

"Let's hope so."

Allu huffed in annoyance at this comment. "And if not, what does it matter? Those people are *traitors.*"

"Let's hope so," Ned told her.

31

Two days later, Ned and Allu set off once again from the city. Once again they traveled in sleighs with the Song Guards—four captains this time and dozens of troops. Once again teams of runners pulled cargo sleighs loaded with equipment. And on reaching the Lowland, Allu and Ned and the Song Guards once again confronted bands of traitors—far more traitors than earlier—in the towns they entered.

What they saw surprised them. Some towns seemed to have no traitors present but no townspeople either, as if everyone had fled. In other towns, Allu and Ned encounered more traitors than before, not fewer. Far from submitting to the Song Guards, these traitors were resisting. Not only did they refuse to submit when the entourage arrived: they lashed out instead. Some even gathered in the streets and started singing:

> So let us now claim what belongs
> To us, and let us right the wrongs—

Allu couldn't believe they would be so brazen. Worse yet, their treasonous behavior was clearly spreading. She, Ned, and the Song Guards would quence the flames before they exploded into a full conflagration. The Song Guard captains mobilized their troops. Ned deployed his powerful instruments—drums, horns, gongs—to fight back. Once again these instruments jolted the traitors and restrained their actions. Once again the traitors ended up stunned and weakened. Once again Allu, standing near a sleigh, sang in ways that restored full order to the traitors' towns.

Hush my darlings, go to sleep—
Dive into that endless deep.

The traitors fell silent. Having no choice, they listened. Listening, they grew calm. Growing calm, they dispersed, slowed, lay down, and slept.

In other towns, however, Allu and Ned and the Song Guards met with even more resistance. Traitors ran toward them in open farmland, each of these men, women, and children wielding—*instruments*. Allu could scarcely believe what she saw. People played their own drums, flutes, harps, and other devices that they shouldn't have known how to play—that they shouldn't have possessed in the first place! "How did they get these?" she asked Ned.

"I have no idea," he answered. "Perhaps they stole them. Or perhaps"—and here he hesitated—"they made them."

"Made them?"

"Just look."

Allu gazed out toward a scattering of traitors who skulked through a field like wolves preparing to attack a flock of sheep. She grasped Ned's words. The traitors' instruments had been built from ordinary items. These villagers had tranformed copper pots into gongs. Wooden boxes into drums. Metal tubes into flutes. She felt astonished that such ignorant people had somehow fashioned their own instruments; at the same time, she felt rage that they would have dared to. A short distance ahead, more than a dozen traitors now faced Ned, Allu, and the Song Guards. The traitors massed to form a little squadron, they readied their instruments, and they played. The tune wafting forth was crude and strange, more noise than melody, but its sound was intense and powerful. It resembled the cry of a wild and powerful bird, a creature long accustomed to hiding in the woods but now emerging into the open. She felt dizzy as she heard it wash through her.

Listening, Allu wanted to shout out at them: You have no right! She wanted, if nothing else, to laugh at such preposterous music. She didn't. She couldn't. What the traitors played wasn't beautiful, but it possessed vitality and confidence that she couldn't ignore. It had a strange, raw energy.

Allu felt weak and weary as she listened. Ned and the Song Guards, too, looked almost ill as they heard the same music. The traitors' songs, though primitive and strange, clearly possessed a dangerous power. Not enough, and not for long. Listening, Allu tolerated this assault briefly, took a deep breath, and counterattacked.

> Dive into that gentle lake—
> Go to sleep and never wake.

The effect was immediate. The traitors listened. They paused. They faltered. They crouched and lay down.

They slept.

32

"Why are we putting all these people to sleep?" Allu asked the High Master two days later, once the expeditionary force had returned to Sifirithi.

The Master laughed warmly at this question. "Allu, dear child—isn't it obvious?"

"Not entirely."

"When people are asleep," the Master said, "they can't complain. They can't cause trouble. Best of all, they can't fight."

"Which makes them—harmless?"

"Completely harmless."

Allu contemplated these words uneasily.

Before she could speak again, however, the Master went on: "In this way you have performed a great service to the Realm, to Sifirithi, and to the Harmonor. What had been harmful is now harmless. The traitors' treason has failed."

"That's good," said Allu, unsure what else to say.

"Very good indeed. Especially because you were able to take action even where we least expected to encounter trouble."

"Excuse me?" Allu wasn't sure what she meant.

"In the last of the towns you visited."

Allu felt a twinge of alarm. "What town do you mean?" Allu asked.

"None of any consequence, as you above all would know."

Now a chill passed through her flesh. "What town?"

"A pointless little peasant town called Laro."

VIII

THE LAST ANTHEM

33

Sitting in his workshop, Ned gazed out toward the city and the snowfall sifting down upon it. He could scarcely force himself to stay awake, so weary did he feel, yet some kind of agitation kept him from his bed. He shouldn't sleep yet anyway, he told himself: night was still a few hours distant. Better to sit here. Better to contemplate the past few days. The journey to the Lowland. The stops at so many villages. The conflicts with all those traitors—hundreds of them! The sights and sounds of their lashing out with instruments and songs. The same outcome after each skirmish: the traitors submerged in a deep sleep. And then, following all these successes, another trip back to Sifirithi, where once again Ned, Allu, and the Song Guards met with great acclaim.

Such was their victory.

Or was it victory?

He jolted on hearing a knock at his door. Ned held off from answering. Maybe the noise was just the wind. Then the knocking started once again, now louder. He sprang up, crossed the workshop, and pulled open the door.

Allu stood there on the landing.

"Oh!" he exclaimed.

Without comment she stepped into the room. Snow covered her cloak. Ned watched her ease out of it. He took the garment, shook off the snow, and hung the cloak on a hook.

Allu, silent before him in her bell cloth robe, offered no greeting. But then at once a torrent of words burst forth: "You were right. I was wrong. What a fool I've been! We've done a terrible deed, both of us, using our music against these people. *My* people, I might add. The last of the villages we visited and suppressed was my own. It was Laro.

Who knows?—my own family may have been among the people I put to sleep. People who now remain asleep. Ned, what have we done? What have I done?"

"We didn't know," he told her, hoping to ease her distress.

"*You* knew, or seemed to know. You said as much. Yet I wouldn't listen—wouldn't believe you."

"You believe me now."

"I do."

He motioned for her to come into the room and warm herself by the fire. Allu couldn't stop shaking, she was so cold. Or was it fear, not snow and wind, that chilled her?

She wouldn't sit. She paced near the hearth like a caged beast. "We have to leave. We have to flee."

"But flee to where?" he asked, feeling desolate.

"Anywhere. The Lowland. Some other place."

"The Masters will notice."

"Let them notice. We'll be long gone."

"They'll follow us."

"Those old men and women? They can scarcely walk unassisted!"

"They'll send the Song Guards."

"Let the Song Guards follow us, then. They'll never catch us. And if they do, you'll stun them with your instruments."

"My instruments are all too large to take."

"Not the flute. Bring your flute! You'll stun them—and then I'll put them to sleep."

"Allu—"

"We must. Tonight!"

"It's too dangerous."

"Staying is too dangerous," Allu insisted. "Can't you see? The longer we wait, the more people in the realm will be helpless—as helpless as sleeping babies. Then all will be lost."

Falling silent, Ned thought over Allu words. She was right: they had waited long enough. Too long. He saw no alternative to her plan.

Just then a knock startled them. They gazed at each other but couldn't speak.

The knocking turned into pounding.

"Ignore it!" Allu whispered.

Ned couldn't move. Then, just as he noticed he'd left the latch unbolted, the handle below it turned abruptly. The door swung open.

On the other side stood Dessina. She looked at Ned and Allu for a long moment. Then she walked into the room, shut the door firmly, and brushed the snow off her shoulders and arms. "I apologize for interrupting your little parley," she told Ned, ignoring Allu, "but you and I must have one of our own."

"I can't," Ned stated.

"No? Too busy chirping with your little songbird?"

"Please leave."

"That's not an acceptable request," Dessina said. "Not when I'm your betrothed and you are mine. Not when we'll be married in a few days' time."

"I'm asking you to leave."

Now Dessina turned at last to Allu. "The person who should leave is this one—this rough-feathered sparrow."

Ned felt both relieved and alarmed when Allu said, "I will leave only if Ned asks me to."

"You have no say in this matter," Dessina told her.

"It's *his* say," Allu told her. "This is Ned's workshop."

"True enough, but Ned lives and works here only with the Masters' permission."

"Maybe so, but you aren't a Master."

Now Dessina smiled. "I needn't be a Master. I have my Master's ear. He listens to me. The other Masters listen to him. And if I tell them what I suspect about you two—what I know—then the Harmonor, too, will—"

"Go," Ned told her. "Leave at once. You have no business here. You weary me. You sicken me."

"You are my betrothed."

"I would rather marry a snowdrift than you," he stated, trembling.

These words silenced her. He saw anger, hurt, and shock in Dessina's eyes.

"Very well, then," she said at last. "Marry your snowdrift. I wish you a chilly time in her embrace." She turned, pulled open the door, and left.

34

Allu and Ned stared at each other for a moment, then moved quickly to prepare. Allu watched Ned stride over to a shelf and locate his flute. At once she raided the workshop's pantry for bread and cheese to take on their voyage. Placing these items in a leather bag she found on the floor, Allu crossed the room, took her cloak from its hook by the door, and took down Ned's, too, as he approached her. They put on their cloaks, gloves, and fur caps. They readied their belongings. Without speaking, they descended the staircase and left the tower.

Snow fell thick as fog. Gusty wind made the snowfall look still thicker. Allu could have sung the Anthem to Disperse Blizzards, of course, but she held off: this storm would be their veil. Best of all, the harsh weather had driven almost everyone else indoors. Allu and Ned rushed down the empty lane.

"We can't leave by the main gate," Ned told her, "but there's another one not far away."

Before they had taken more than a few steps, however, Allu spotted a squad of Song Guards right ahead. She warned Ned: "Look."

He motioned to his left.

Allu saw the entrance to a narrow alleyway. She and Ned ran over to it, entered, and strode off as quickly as the snowfall would allow. At times they had to grope their way forward through the storm. On reaching a wider street, they made faster progress.

Allu ran faster than she thought possible. The stone lane underfoot was slick with snow, so she slipped now and then but somehow avoided falling. Down staircases and alleyways, faster and faster, almost too fast to stay on their feet, Allu and Ned ran away. She wasn't confident of Ned's plan. She followed him anyway. It didn't matter where they went, she told herself, just so long as she never heard the Masters' music again . . . so long as she never sang another lullaby. This was the wrong music! The anthems and lullabies were mistaken, false, nothing but lies! Powerful, of course: definitely powerful. But power made no difference, it left her cold and frightened, since power was just another lie: a rose with a wasp inside. Breathless, Allu kept remembering those people in Laro and what she had done to them. Laro!

Then at once she heard the chimes of Sifirithi start to ring all around her. She tried not to listen but couldn't help but hear the calming notes. She and Ned slowed, paused, took a few more steps, and stopped. Ned looked at her. She looked at him. Allu felt as if winter had suddenly thawed; summer had bloomed. Music swirled around them like warm wind. The wrong music? she asked herself. How could this music be wrong? She felt lighter than a dandelion puff riding the breeze. Allu started to wonder if perhaps she were mistaken. How could she doubt these people? How could she question the Masters? Allu, a mere villager: how could she claim to know more than the Masters? She stood there feeling shameful.

Just then another squad of Song Guards turned a corner a short distance away. They halted. Several pointed up the lane toward Allu and Ned. This sight was alarming anyway, but all the more so when Allu spotted Dessina among the Guards.

"They're the ones!" she shouted, pointing at Ned and Allu.

The expression Allu saw on Ned's face now showed more than alarm: hurt, too, and something like disgust.

"You there, Lowlander!" cried out one of the Song Guards. "And you: Ned Jerosso! Stop at once!"

Allu was appalled to see Dessina guiding the Song Guards. Such a manipulative vixen! Yet while hearing the chimes' calm music, she also felt an urge to walk down the lane, greet the Song Guards, and embrace them. The chimes of Sifirithi rang and rang. Allu listened. Be calm, they told her, be simple, they said, and above all *obey*.

Allu stood there meekly. The Song Guards rushed up the street.

They had almost reached Allu and Ned when Allu's own music came back to her. She scarcely heard the voices at first: only the smallest wisps of a melody. Allu ignored them. More music was the last thing she needed. Then it grew louder. It demanded her attention. She forced herself to listen. When the chimes of Sifirithi almost drowned her own music, Allu struggled to hear it. She cupped her hands against her ears to block out the chimes.

At that moment she noticed still another melody: the Song Guards, now standing just a few paces away, had begun singing the Anthem to Subdue Runaways.

> Stop, you renegades! Your flight is done!
> Submit! Submit! Submit! Submit!—
> As night submits to the rising sun!

Allu and Ned set off at once, running hard, slipping and skittering in the snow but somehow able to keep ahead of the people chasing them.

"Stop!" shouted one of the Song Guards. "Come back here!"

"Come back—we mean no harm!" called out another.

"We will live together in harmony!" proclaimed a third.

Ignoring them, Allu and Ned turned each corner fast, hoping to escape. There seemed to be more Song Guards each time Allu turned back to look.

They found themselves abruptly face to face with yet another squad—eight Song Guards in an alley—who started singing the Anthem to Capture Outlaws. Allu and Ned tried to escape but couldn't. The Guards sang loudly. Allu slowed and stopped. She saw Ned, too, falter as the music took hold of them. Allu felt her arms and legs grow weak and heavy. She felt as if she weighed a thousand pounds. She wanted to sit. She wanted to lie down. She wanted to give up and never run off again. Then, to her surprise, she saw Ned remove his flute from inside his cloak, and she heard him play a melody that stunned the Song Guards. The melody slithered out of the flute, coiled itself, then rose and reared back, hissing, as if ready to strike. The Song Guards, clearly fearful, staggered away. Allu and Ned pushed past them and up the street.

They now ran from dozens of people. Allu didn't know if she and Ned could escape, or how, or where they would go, but they ran anyway. The music these people sang to restrain Allu and Ned only prodded them. The wrong music! She knew that now without a flicker of doubt. It was false, powerful but false, and dangerous. Allu understood now because the real music welled up inside her and told her so. Voices grew loud inside her and made her listen.

Even as more and more people chased them—some shouting, some singing—Allu kept hearing her own music and kept listening to it. She wanted to protect herself and Ned. She wanted to protect the people out there in the realm. She feared that her voice might fall silent. Fighting this fear, Allu ran faster and faster, helped Ned when he fell, accepted his help when she slipped, rushed through the city, passed through the low places, then started up the other mountain. She paid no attention to the Song Guards when they called out to her, pleaded with her, sang to her. All she did was listen to her own music. Somehow, as Allu and Ned climbed the steep, slick path and saw how quickly they left everyone else behind, she knew that those voices would be safe inside her.

35

Ned took notice of his surroundings. He and Allu slowed and stopped.

Nobody followed them now, and no wonder: they had almost reached the top of the highest mountain in Sifirithi. Ned stood still, gasping for breath, and tried to decide their next move. At least the Song Guards hadn't pursued them further. He could hear the squadrons far below, however, when some notes from their anthems wafted up through the snowfall. Somehow their unwillingness to follow worried Ned rather than reassuring him. Even the Song Guards feared this place.

"Where are we?" Allu asked.

"I think you know," he told her.

All of Sifirithi now lay below: the Square, the houses around the Square, the streets and corridors and bridges, the buildings huddled close to the mountainside, the Low, Middle, and High Towers. Even the stormclouds now lay below them. Ned could also see snow-covered hills rising in the distance and the Lowland beyond the hills. He and Allu stared as if in a trance. He could guess Allu's thoughts. Somewhere out there was Laro. Where? How far away? No doubt she was wondering if she would ever go home again . . . if she would ever see her family at all.

Ned struggled with his own thoughts and worries. His parents . . . Were they safe? He had no idea what to think. No idea—until he saw Allu, proceeding out of confidence or rage, now starting up the path again toward the summit. Ned hesitated a moment, then followed her.

A palace rose from the mountaintop. At first Ned thought this palace must have been made of ice. Harsh winter sunlight shone so hard on the walls that Ned squinted, shaded his eyes, and turned away. Then he looked again and saw that the entire palace was, in fact, made of glass. Not just his eyes, but also his ears, told him so. So many pieces of glass dangled everywhere—from the roof, the balconies, the eaves, the windows—that the palace clinked and tinkled like a gigantic set of chimes whenever the wind came through. *The palace was made of music.* Ned and Allu stopped, stood right there in the path, and listened, unable to think or act.

When they came to their senses, they walked the rest of the way. They reached the front stairs and started climbing them: pure glass. They walked up to the door: also glass.

Allu, opening the door without knocking, went inside.

Ned followed at once.

A tall man stood ten or twelve paces from the doorway. "So: here you are," he said. "Late, but still in good time."

Neither Allu nor Ned could speak. Ned himself tried responding to the man's words but couldn't. His appearance took Ned's voice away. Although he wore full robes, just like the Masters, his garments weren't stick-cloth or even bell-cloth but were something else altogether. Thousands of tiny glass pendants hung from its folds, over-lapping like fish-scales, so that the whole robe seemed to be glass; his head wore a cap covered with little glass pendants; and even as the man just stood there, all of those pendants released more delicate notes than any of the chimes outside. Ned watched and listened. The man watched back. Ned felt afraid: he was helpless to do more than watch and listen. Late afternoon sunlight came in through the open doorway and made the man radiant. He sparkled like a tree after an ice storm. Tiny rainbows flickered around him. And the music he made while simply standing there was the sweetest Ned had ever heard. Perfect harmony! All Ned could say was, "We tried to come sooner."

"No matter. Everything happens in good time." Then the man beckoned. Even that one gesture made his glass chimes release a torrent of little notes.

"Who are you?" Allu asked.

The man smiled. His teeth looked so white and perfect that Ned expected them to ring like crystal. He said, "You know who."

Ned was appalled to grasp that after so many years of hearing stories about this man, only now did he stand before him face to face. "The Harmonor."

"Yes, my children. I am the Harmonor."

Then he walked off, filling the air with whispered melodies. Allu and Ned, following reluctantly, sought that music like hungry people following the scent of food. Although Ned told himself to be careful, he felt compelled to follow. The same was true for Allu: she, too, followed. They felt the Harmonor's music pull them into its current and, like a chilly stream, sweep them away.

They arrived at a great hall. The Harmonor smiled when his young guests looked around, struck mute by what they saw. The entire room was made of glass. Light coming through the walls sent wisps of color shooting in every direction. Ned felt as small and helpless as a spider on a chandelier. The Harmonor said, "Please sit." He motioned to some glass chairs. "We must get better acquainted."

Allu spoke first. "What do you want from us?"

"Come. Sit with me."

"What do you want?" Ned asked.

The Harmonor sat carefully. Despite his care, his sitting made the sound of someone dropping diamonds on a marble floor. "Do not be impatient, my children. You will know everything in good time."

"We're not children," Allu told him. "Certainly not *your* children."

"No? Perhaps you are."

"My parents live in Laro."

"You can have more than two parents. Some parents create children with their bodies. Some with their minds. Some, it seems, with their voices. You are my child, Allu, in more ways than you know. You as well, Ned Jerosso."

"Not in *any* way!" Allu stated, raising her voice. *"None!"*

Though Ned felt angry too, he kept quiet, fearful of enraging the Harmonor.

The man smiled, then said: "When you came to me, Allu, you were nothing. None of the Masters would believe you could do more than cheep like a chickadee. They wanted to send you back to the Lowland. I told them to keep you here. At my command they fed you, clothed you, and helped you prove yourself."

"Which I did," Allu said confidently.

The Harmonor nodded. "Indeed you did. You began your training. You learned well. The Masters taught you how to sing and what to sing. You sang better than we thought possible—sang so well that you soon learned everything. Everything except for what I myself can teach you." Before Ned could interrupt, the Harmonor turned to him as if to answer an unasked question. "And you, Ned Jerosso. Didn't I rescue you as well from the Lowland? Didn't I arrange to bring you here, feed you, raise you, train you? Didn't I have the Masters teach you everything possible? So much, in fact, that you are now the finest builder of instruments?"

Before Ned could answer, Allu spoke abruptly: "What do you want from us?"

"I want to continue what the Masters have begun, my child."

"Don't call me your child."

When the Harmonor raised a hand as if in objection, his chimes gave a sudden jingle. "I transformed you from a country sparrow into a bird of paradise. Is this not fatherhood?"

"No."

"Then you are ungrateful."

"I'm grateful for what you have given me, not for what was already mine."

"*Nothing* was yours."

"I've always sung," she told him. "You didn't give me that."

Ned winced to hear these words. Allu would enrage the Harmonor, would cause him to punish both Ned and Allu. Yet he admired Allu's bravery in rebuffing this man's arrogant words.

The Harmonor seemed ready to punish them—his pale gray eyes narrowed—but he restrained himself. He smiled. "There is no need to argue. Let me explain. I only wish to share something with you."

"Share something?" Ned asked. "What would you share?"

Gesturing around him, the Harmonor said, "My land. My power. I would share Sifirithi, Siir, and all the people who live here in the Realm."

Allu looked ready to lash back. Ned felt great relief when she restrained herself. She asked only: "Why would you share anything with us?"

"Even the most powerful king must have an heir." The Harmonor continued before Ned or Allu could object. "Yes, an heir. You two have proved yourself beyond my wildest expectations. You will keep proving yourself, too, I'm sure of it. Both of you. Who better to take my place when the time is ready?"

"You want us to *help* you?" Allu said, her voice full of astonishment.

"Precisely. Much as you yourselves have helped me. We will help one another."

Allu was clearly pondering these words. She said, "Help one another . . ."

Ned felt uneasy about what was happening. At first Allu had pushed back against the Harmonor; now her tone was softer. He couldn't understand her intentions.

"Maybe we *can* help you," she continued. "Maybe we have more to learn."

Did she have a strategy? Was she playing along? Was she just pretending to cooperate?

"More than you can imagine," the Harmonor told her. "How to sing mud into gold. How to sing night into day. How to sing hate," he said, "into love."

Ned could see this man watching them closely.

"Hate into love?" Allu asked.

The Harmonor continued. "Think of it. From this mountaintop, you can see all of Siir. The people living there, the animals, the farms and meadows, even the rivers and lakes will be yours. Everyone will honor you. Everyone will worship you. Of course," he said, his voice dropping, "some traitors still remain in several of the villages. As the two of you have proved, however, traitors are powerless before the melodies you sing and the instruments you play." The Harmonor stared at them. His glass robes jingled so faintly that Ned leaned forward to hear them better. "Sifirithi rules Siir. You two will someday rule Sifirithi."

Ned forced back the confusion rising within him. Sifirithi! Siir! Yet he couldn't forget those traitors in the Lowland. The bloody, dust-covered men. The stumbling, haggard women. The terrified children. Those people were just villagers, neighbors, perhaps members of Allu's own family. What of them?

The Harmonor said, "You possess great gifts. Use them wisely."

Ned wanted more time—time to think, time to understand these words. He didn't know what to say. This man's words weren't what he had expected. It seemed risky to refuse him, yet Ned feared accepting.

The Harmonor's chimes started up again: simple and complex as a roosting flock of birds singing to one another at sunset.

When Allu gave Ned a sidelong glance, he started to grasp her intentions. The plan was so simple that he almost laughed when he understood. Not betrayal, but trickery! Playing along, they would gain this man's confidence, would acquire his power, would take their time turning it against him. She looked pensive for a moment, then said,

"I'll do it. I want to learn from you. I want to learn everything. Teach me."

"I shall," said the Harmonor, looking pleased. He turned to Ned. "And you?"

Ned told him, "Teach me too."

The Harmonor smiled. "A wise decision."

"Thank you!" Allu exclaimed, her voice heavy with gratitude. "Thank you so much!"

When she saw the Harmonor stand, Allu stood also.

Ned faltered for a moment, then joined them.

The Harmonor said, "You understand now. There is no reason for distrust."

Allu said, "We do apologize."

"Never mind. You are cautious. That is good. Now: come with me. We must celebrate." The Harmonor reached out and took Allu by the hand.

Ned followed.

Without hesitating, they went with him deeper into the palace. Ned saw three servants approach, each attired in a white robe, one of them carrying a tray. When these servants reached Allu, Ned, and the Harmonor, they presented goblets to the girl, the boy, and the man.

The Harmonor raised his goblet. "To Sifirithi!" he proclaimed. "To Siir! To the music binding us together in perfect harmony!"

Allu raised her glass and tapped it against the Harmonor's with a delicate ping.

Ned did the same.

The three of them chanted together: "Sifirithi! Siir! Music!"

Together they drank.

36

After saying farewell to the Harmonor, Allu and Ned left with his servants. Together they walked through the palace—down torch-lit corridors, across a great hall, down still more corridors—until they reached a stairway.

"Where are we going?" Allu asked.

"Into the mountain," replied one of the servants. "The mountain is full of rooms. There will be a cozy place for you both."

That staircase, made of glass like everything else in the Harmonor's court, glowed as if illuminated from within. Allu marvelled at their radiance. The sound, too, pleased her: notes that Allu's bell cloth robe released now echoed up and down until the entire staircase flowed with her music.

She turned to Ned, who was following her, and she smiled.

He smiled back.

They descended for a long time. Allu stepped with great care, though she felt so excited that she could have run headlong toward her destination. Somehow, almost without effort, she and Ned had gotten what they wanted. They had won. Allu had tricked the Harmonor. Best of all, she and Ned had prevailed without a struggle. Allu and Ned would go along with his plan, would learn what he taught them, would take over Sifirithi. Within a few months? Weeks? It hardly mattered. All that mattered was fooling the Harmonor and gaining his power. Then Allu and Ned would free everyone in Siir.

She noticed at about that time how the staircase was growing dimmer: much less light reached the depths into which Allu, Ned, and the servants were now descending. She peered into the spiral of stairs below. She couldn't see much more than shadows. "Will we arrive soon?" she asked.

"Soon," one of the servants replied.

With great relief she saw light below her. She hurried toward it. Allu reached a doorway. She pulled back the glass door.

Hands on the other side grabbed her at once. Two guards—huge men—took hold of Allu by the arms and dragged her away.

Stumbling and tripping, she shouted, "Wait! You don't understand! I'm Allu! Wait!"

She could hear Ned, too, struggling with someone right behind her.

"We have waited long enough," answered the bigger of the guards. The other one laughed at her. Wearing ragged leather pants and tunics, they smelled like spoiled meat.

Allu looked backward. Two other guards gripped Ned tightly. The white-robed servants stood watching from beside the doorway. Only when Allu cried out did they smile.

One of Allu's captors said, "Come along."

Allu would have fought back, pulled away, and struck them, but somehow she felt too bewildered to fight. When she glanced back at Ned, she saw him looking stunned and helpless.

The guards marched them forward.

She saw at once that this place was a prison. The room was full of cages, each holding a prisoner, yet the cages weren't just cages. Allu noticed one of the prisoners watching her from behind bars, but the bars were long, thin wires, so that the man looked like someone sitting behind a harp, or rather several harps, with wires surrounding him on all sides. While sitting there, he clutched at the wires desperately, plucking them. Allu slowed and stopped. Sad music reached her from that cage as the prisoner inside it played a random melody.

Now Allu fought back. She pulled away from the guards, kicked them, punched them, did everything possible to escape. She could see Ned, too, fighting back. His guards quickly overpowered him. Allu's guards just laughed as they restrained her.

"Let go of me! I'm Allu—you have the wrong person!"

The big guard said, "If you are Allu, we have exactly who we want."

"You have the wrong place!" Ned shouted. "This is a prison!"

"Indeed—the prison for musical traitors. Would you like to meet them?" he asked, gesturing toward the cages they now approached.

"These are the traitors who played harps even though all harps are banned."

"I never played a harp!"

"Meet the others, then."

The guards walked so fast that Allu and Ned could scarcely keep up with them. At times the four men simply carried their captives by clutching both Allu and Ned under the arms like farmers lifting sacks of potatoes.

When they passed another row of cages, Allu saw prisoners stirring inside them. A few rushed forth to look. Others sat passively. Still others wailed and moaned. What she saw made Allu desperate to escape. Fear rose inside her: these prisoners looked helpless, frantic, crazy— shadow-eyed phantoms. Some of them reached out to her and Ned as they passed. Others called out. One of them wailed, "All is lost! Lost! The Harmonor will sing the Last Anthem!"

Allu asked, "What is the Last Anthem?"

"Nothing that concerns you," said one of the guards. "Just come along."

The prisoner cried out again: "He will sing the Last Anthem!"

Now Allu saw cages even more hideous than the first. A cage made of metal tubes that tolled dully as the prisoner inside rolled back and forth . . . A cage made of wooden blocks that clattered and clacked when the captive within it whacked them . . . A cage made of a big brass bell that rang as the prisoner, dangling there like a clapper, thrashed about . . . Each cage seemed more terrible than the previous. The noise was intense.

"Don't lock us up!" Allu told the guards.

"We're sorry!" Ned exclaimed. "We didn't do anything wrong. Let us talk with the Harmonor again—just don't put us in cages!"

"We will put you where the Harmonor wants you."

"Not in such a noisy place," Allu said.

The guard laughed. "Nowhere so noisy. Not with these traitors, certainly—the ones who rang bells though all bells are forbidden."

"I didn't ring bells."

One guard told her, "You will be happy, then, in your quiet place."

"Very quiet," said the other.

They proceeded another half-dozen paces and stopped. The first guard said, "The quietest place of all."

Somehow Allu felt relieved to leave so much commotion behind. She forced herself to be calm. She and Ned would be alone at last. They would figure out what to do. One of the guards held her while another fumbled with some keys, struggled with the lock, and at last opened a huge door. It swung back, grunting. The shadows parted. Allu peered into the room.

She saw a stone floor and, opposite, a damp stone wall. "No!" she protested.

The guard with the keys said, "You wanted a quiet place."

The other guard laughed loudly.

"Not this!" Ned shouted behind her.

"Nothing could be quieter."

"Wait!"

"It is you who will wait."

Before Allu could move or speak, the guards shoved her headlong into that room. She fell at once. The guards flung Ned in too. Allu got up, then fell again on the icy floor. Dazed, she heard the door slam.

She lay there a while. The stone felt cold and damp to the touch. Silence blanketed her, bundled her. She shouted for help, screamed, pleaded for help—

Ned, too, shouted.

They shouted until, exhausted, they gave up and just clung to each other in silence.

37

Ned awoke shivering. He couldn't remember what had happened or why he felt so cold. He looked around. Darkness. He reached out, touched the damp wall, and remembered. Furious, he stood up but fell at once.

He lay there wondering what to do. A sudden jangle of tiny bells surprised him. How could she have forgotten! "Allu?"

"Ned!" Her voice was little more than a whisper.

"Are you hurt?"

"I don't think so—just cold. Freezing cold!"

Ned reached out in the darkness. To his left he touched bell cloth—Allu. He felt her cold fingers touch his hand. Ned pulled himself closer. They held each other and delighted in the warmth they shared.

"What can we do?" he asked. "We're trapped."

Her reply was immediate. "I'll sing my way out."

"Sing?"

"I'll tear this prison apart with anthems. I'll smash the stones and rip open the cages."

"Allu—"

"I'll wreck the whole city."

Ned felt dismayed to hear how weak, how fragile, Allu's voice sounded.

"The Song Guards will flee," she whispered. "The Masters will tremble. The Harmonor will weep and plead for mercy."

"What's wrong with your voice?" Ned asked.

She ignored his question. "I'll start with the Anthem to Open Locked Doors."

When she tried to sing the first note, however, nothing happened. Ned heard little more than a sigh.

Allu tried again.

Still nothing.

"Maybe the Anthem to Melt Ice," she whispered. She took a deep breath and sang. Nothing happened. Allu started coughing and couldn't stop for a long time.

Ned felt more and more alarmed. Allu could scarcely speak, much less sing.

She tried the Anthem to Calm Panic and Fear, then the Anthem to Ward Off Worries. Nothing. "Let me warm up first," she told Ned. Allu tried singing the Anthem to Soothe a Sore Throat. When she couldn't sing a single note, she gave up, weary and scared. She gave a last try: one of the simple Low Choir exercises. In a dry whisper she said, *"The Harmonor's wine."*

Ned felt sick on hearing these words. Of course: the Harmonor had put some kind of poison in Allu's goblet.

"There's no hope," she said.

At that moment a voice spoke somewhere in the darkness: "Don't give up just yet."

Ned gagged on his own fear. That voice spoke from just a short distance away. Too scared to move, he blurted out, *"Who is it?"*

A match flared. In the yellow light Ned saw an old man: the lean face, the wispy beard.

Allu rasped out his name—"Sorrik!"—and reached toward him at once.

The match fell from the old man's hands. Darkness closed in again. Ned heard the thuds and grunts of two people bumping into each other.

"Careful!" said the old man's voice.

Then another match flared, revealing Sorrik in the yellow light.

"What are you doing here?" Ned asked.

"Waiting for you."

"You, too, are in prison?"

Sorrik raised a candle. He held the match to the wick, let the flame take hold, and blew out the match. "Unlike you," he said, "I suspected what would happen. I was ready."

Allu whispered, "I don't understand—how did you get here? This is all so strange."

"Strange: yes, very strange," Sorrik replied, "but simpler than you think. Allu, I could guess where you would both end up. I even guessed that you two would end up in this very cell. Had I been wrong, however, I would have found you anyway." Sorrik reached to one side and lifted something from the shadows: a ring of big brass keys. He jingled them.

The sound was sweeter than all the chimes in Sifirithi.

Allu laughed in delight—or tried, since her laugh was almost silent. She whispered, "Sorrik, I'm so glad you've come! Now help us escape!"

The old man nodded slowly but didn't speak.

"Sorrik, *now!*"

"Not so fast—"

"The Harmonor is preparing to destroy us!"

"I know," said the old emissary.

After a moment's pause, Allu said, "You *do* know. You've known all along. Why didn't you tell me?"

"I tried, Allu."

"But—sooner."

"I wasn't sure sooner. And if I'd spoken, you would never have believed me."

"Sorrik, what are we going to do?"

The old man sat staring at the candle. Its flame wavered; the walls shifted with the light. "In the past I wouldn't have believed this turn of events," he told her. "The Harmonor came to power long ago and brought order to Sifirithi. Imagine! With the music he taught us, trouble fled like a thief. Discomfort fled, too. Hunger, sickness, and weakness took flight as well. The Harmonor's music gave these ills no choice but to flee. As he trained the Masters, they in turn trained everyone else, until the people of Sifirithi lived in perfect harmony."

"But in Siir—"

"Let me finish. In Siir, people lived their lives like people everywhere: working, loving, hating, struggling, celebrating, grieving. But since the Harmonor knew a better way, he banned the people's music and used his own throughout the land. Soon there would be no sorrow, envy, anger, or impatience anywhere in Siir."

"No joy or hope, either," said Allu.

"That's obvious now. As I told you, I never thought our lives would turn out as they have."

"Anybody in the Lowland could have told you."

Sorrik shook his head. "We thought it was all for the best—for the good of Sifirithi, for the good of Siir. All in harmony."

Ned felt shocked when Allu spoke out in anger: "You should at least have suspected. Instead, you did what the Harmonor wanted. You did what the Masters asked. You went down into the Lowland and brought back young people to teach. For the good of Siir! More like for the *Harmonor's* good—and his alone!"

"Forgive me."

"Sorrik, you should be ashamed of yourself."

"Please forgive me."

"Think of the harm you've done!"

"You must understand," said the old emissary, reaching out to her. "I never wanted to harm anyone. I believed I was doing good deeds, not evil. I went to the villages looking for people who could sing the best, who could bring forth kindness from a cruel man's heart and generosity from a miser's."

"It didn't work out that way."

"Allu: when I first heard you sing, I wept for joy. You sang like no one else. You sang songs like no others. Like none I had imagined. I told myself, These songs are what we need. These songs are what we have waited for. These songs—"

"I made them up. They're just songs."

"Beautiful songs."

"Just songs."

Sorrik said, "You must sing your songs, Allu. They could soften even the Harmonor's heart."

Ned felt fear seep through his body. How would Allu sing? She was nearly mute.

Then Allu herself expressed Ned's fears: "I can't sing. The Harmonor served me wine that took my voice away. I can't sing at all."

"You must try."

"I already tried."

"Try again."

She opened her mouth and made one last attempt. Not a single note came forth. "It's no use," she said.

The emissary watched her, then looked down at the keys resting in his lap. He shook his head. "Then all is lost. I have learned that many people hate the Harmonor—almost everyone, in fact—though they scarcely know it themselves. They would all happily be rid of him. But few have stood up to him till now. Only you have revealed a power that could defeat him. Everyone else is helpless. Now you are as helpless as the rest." After a moment's pause he said once more: "All is lost."

38

Listening to these words, Allu felt her own hope burn and dwindle into ashes. She gazed at the old man: motionless, silent, empty. She felt as old and tired as Sorrik. She turned to Ned: sitting nearby but watching her so sadly that he seemed clear across the world.

Then, without knowing what she meant, Allu said, "If I can't sing now, maybe someone else can sing for me."

"There is no one else," Ned told her.

"Not true—there are many."

Sorrik seemed to perk up. "The prisoners?"

"The prisoners."

At once they all got up and rushed to the door. But Sorrik took hold of Allu's arm and, stopping her, said, "What about the guards?"

Allu laughed. "Tricking them shouldn't be too difficult."

"Maybe not—but still dangerous."

Sorrik walked back to the corner and returned with the keyring. He tried several keys, found the right one, unlocked the door, and waited a moment. "I shall go first."

The emissary eased open the door, its hinges stuttering. Allu half-expected to hear shouts and footsteps but didn't—only the distant clatter and clang of the musical prisoners. Dim light drifted into the cell. After hesitating, Sorrik leaned out and peered around the corner. He motioned for Allu and Ned to follow.

They obeyed him eagerly. Although frightened, Allu felt ready for whatever faced them now. Anything to stop the Harmonor! Sorrik eased through the corridor; Allu and Ned came after. Each step brought them closer to the light and the prisoners' din.

When Sorrik stopped, Allu and Ned stopped too. The old man gazed out of the shadows toward the room full of cages. Allu waited, restless. Ned seemed more and more uneasy as he saw what they faced. Then the emissary turned to them. "My eyes are weak," he whispered. "Both of you must look and tell me what you see."

Allu let Sorrik ease back; then she took his place and sized up the room.

The four guards stood not far away. Neither showed any sign of noticing Allu, Ned, and Sorrik. After a few moments they turned and walked off slowly.

Allu said, "Guards—but only a few. They appear to be leaving."

"Let's move quickly," Sorrik told them. "Take a key, each of you. We'll run to the cages and release as many prisoners as possible." He removed two big brass keys from the ring and gave one to Ned, the other to Allu.

Allu rushed out, reached the nearest cage, and unlocked it. The prisoner inside started shouting, "Please spare me!"

"Hush!" Allu whispered. "I'm not a guard!" She pulled open the door.

Instead of emerging, the prisoner just pulled back.

"What are you waiting for?" Allu asked him. "Hurry! You're a free man!" When he stared at her, unmoving, Allu reached in through the doorway, took hold of his thin wrist, and pulled him out.

Ned did the same with the prisoner in a nearby cage.

Others came forth eagerly. Allu and Ned ran from cage to cage releasing prisoners. Allu could see Sorrik releasing people too. Some of them rushed forth at once, a few hesitated, and some wouldn't come out at all. One of them cried, "All is lost!"

Allu fumbled with the lock to his cage.

"The Harmonor will sing the Last Anthem!"

Just then Allu heard a loud voice from the other room—"You: what are you doing?"—and she saw the guards rushing toward her.

"All is lost!" cried the prisoner.

Angry now, Allu decided to leave him there to wail and moan.

The guards arrived at that moment. So many prisoners had already escaped, however, that they swarmed and overwhelmed their captors. Clusters of women, men, and children grabbed the guards and shoved them into two big cages. Sorrik, Allu, and Ned slammed the doors shut and locked the locks.

"Let me out!" yelled one of the guards.

"Release us!" shouted another.

"The Harmonor will sing you to death!" cried out the third.

Allu turned back to the other cages. Prisoners were now reaching out and pleading for freedom. She set to work with her key. Ned and Sorrik did the same. One after another they opened the locks. Big and little, wood and metal, harp and bell and drum-like cages: each fell open and released the people inside, sometimes two or three at once, until the great hall teemed with prisoners. Soon all of them were free. Allu and Ned then rushed to the next room, where Sorrik had already begun unlocking cages.

Suddenly weary, she faltered. The noise frightened her. All these people running about! So much shouting! Was releasing them a mistake? These prisoners seemed frantic, wild, dangerous. Perhaps the Harmonor was right: they were traitors. But then Allu recalled her brief time in captivity. She conjured an image of the tyrant they were up against. No, they had to gamble. At once she and Ned continued releasing prisoners.

Then something happened that Allu could never have anticipated. A man's voice behind her called out: "Ned!"

Allu assumed that Sorrik had spoken, so she ignored this utterance.

But then a woman's voice called out as well: "Ned! Ned!"

Allu turned to see a remarkable sight: Ned stood before one of the musical cages and stared at two prisoners, a man and a woman, who reached out toward him through the bars. Both wore filthy rags. The woman's long hair looked like long, tangled seaweed. The man's hair was long as well, his beard a matted mess. Ned's expression while gazing at this couple showed his astonishment. *"Mother,"* he said in a bewildered voice. *"Father."*

"Ned!" they both exclaimed again, clearly delighted.

"What are you— I thought—"

"And what are you—?"

Both Ned and his parents fell silent. They simply gazed at one another as jumbled emotions played across their faces. Then Ned unlocked their cage and released them. The parents and the son embraced one another for a long time as Allu and Sorrik watched.

Then, before Allu could interrupt to prod them toward action, Ned himself said, "These are my friends Allu and Sorrik," he told his parents, "and we're freeing all of you prisoners. But we have so little time."

His parents nodded, clearly stunned by this turn of events yet able to grasp the situation. And so they all took action.

Within a short while everyone was out: at least a hundred women, men, and children.

Allu stared at them in amazement. "Listen to me!" she rasped out, her weak voice scarcely audible over all the shouts and laughter. Once again Allu felt afraid. These people looked like beggars and thieves, not musicians! Some were so dirty, so tangled in their filthy rags that they didn't even look like people. She tried catching their attention—"Please listen!"—but the words wouldn't carry.

Sorrik tried calling out too: "We must speak with you!"

"All is lost! Lost!" someone cried out in response.

"The Harmonor is our doom!" someone else shouted.

Allu, Ned, and Sorrik glanced at one another in bewilderment. Allu didn't know what to do. At last she told Ned, "You explain."

He faltered.

"Go ahead," she urged him. "Speak!"

"You're all free now!" Ned shouted to the prisoners. *"Free."*

They must have heard him—people seemed to be listening—yet someone yelled back, *"How* are we free? The Harmonor will sing the Last Anthem."

"Never!" Allu whispered.

Several prisoners shouted, "All is lost!"

Sorrik, too, echoed Allu's cry: "Never!"

"Nothing is lost, believe me," Ned told them, perhaps just making up the words. "We will fight the Harmonor, vanquish the Song Guards, and free all of Siir!"

Once again everyone fell silent. No one moved. Allu almost

expected the prisoners to laugh in disbelief and contempt. A few of them actually did. Then one prisoner, a young man with deep-set eyes and a matted beard, shouted, "Freedom for Siir!"

This battle cry spread at once through the crowd.

"Freedom for Siir!"

"Down with the Harmonor!" someone else called out.

"Freedom for Siir! Down with the Harmonor!"

The crowd grew so angry that Allu and Sorrik backed off.

Then the bearded prisoner raised his hands to the crowd, silenced everyone, and said, "Yes, freedom! But how will we gain it? We have no weapons. We have no tools. We are helpless before the Song Guards. We are at the Harmonor's mercy."

Someone shouted, "Down with the Harmonor!"

"We should bring him down, yes," the bearded man went on, now sadly. "But how can a pack of ragged prisoners bring down the Harmonor? Tell me how." He turned to Allu, Ned, and Sorrik. He stared at them, waiting.

"We can sing," Allu said, her voice little more than a cough.

The same prisoner laughed at her. "Sing? You can scarcely talk!"

Some of the others laughed, too. A murmur swelled from the crowd again.

Allu told them, "*You* sing, then."

"I've never sung in my life!" cried another prisoner, a bent-over little man. "Nor have most of us."

Fearful again, Allu fell silent. She didn't know what to say. She looked over at Ned, then at Sorrik. Neither of them spoke; they just looked back at Allu. Everyone seemed to be waiting for her. Allu asked Sorrik, "What can we tell them?"

"I wish I knew," he replied.

"Don't you have a plan?"

"I thought *you* did."

If she could have sung, Allu would have sung the Anthem to Ease Impatience. But of course she couldn't sing, and she didn't want to sing the Harmonor's music anyway. For once she felt almost relieved to have her voice fail.

"What good are we against the Harmonor?" asked the bearded prisoner. "He can sing us to our death."

Some of the prisoners grew angry. One of them, a woman with tangled hair so long that she kept tripping on it, told Allu, "It's a fine freedom you've given us! We may as well go back to prison!"

Allu looked around. A few of the prisoners did what the woman suggested: they turned, walked away, and climbed back into their cages. Others just stood there looking fearful.

Allu wanted to scream at them. She glanced at Sorrik, but he wouldn't look back. When she tried shouting, she couldn't make a sound. Her voice failed altogether.

She turned to Ned and gazed at him intently.

Ned told her, "Perhaps—" He gestured at the prisoners and their musical cages.

At first Allu wasn't sure what he meant, yet somehow she understood. "Yes, perhaps."

She tried again, this time more gently. "Wait! Please wait," she told the prisoners. "Just give us a little more time. We'll think of something."

39

It was almost dawn by the time Ned, Allu, Sorrik, and the freed prisoners made their way to the surface. After stumbling up many staircases and through many tunnels, everyone had grown weary. Carrying pieces of their cages made them still wearier. Ned himself wanted nothing more than to lie down and sleep, but somehow he pushed ahead anyway. He felt concerned, too, about Allu and Sorrik, both of them clearly exhausted. Ned knew that many of the prisoners were also struggling. He felt most worried about his parents, both of them scarcely able to walk. The noises at his back—stifled weeping, footfalls, echoes, grunts, and sudden cries—reminded Ned of how light his own load was by comparison.

Then, without warning, he saw a rectangle of dim light ahead: a doorway at the end of the corridor.

"We're out," Allu whispered. "We're finally out." She kept walking toward the door.

Ned saw Sorrik reach out to restrain her. "Not so fast," said the old emissary. "We must step carefully until we know where we are."

Sorrik was right; Allu's plan seemed too good to risk. Yet hours of getting organized down in the prison, then hours more of stumbling through the darkness, made it hard for people to restrain their impatience.

Reaching the stone portal, Ned stopped, waited for the others, and peered out into the uncertain light. Night had not fully ended; dawn had not yet arrived. Ned saw everything as if through fog. "Where are we?" he whispered.

"This may be the Compass Gate," the old man replied. "If so, we have reached the Great Circle."

"Just where we want to be," Allu said, her words almost too soft to hear.

"I hope you're right," Ned told her. At once he added: "This is the last place I would have chosen." He couldn't help but recall the fiasco of the avian calliope.

Prisoners had begun gathering behind them by now. With a growing commotion of thumps, rattles, clicks, and clanks, the women and men and children caught up. Ned could see them emerge from the darkness—could see their gray skin, their thin arms and legs, their gaunt faces, their sunken eyes.

Sorrik turned to Allu. "This will be our one chance. If we fail—"

"I'd rather fail than submit," she told him.

"But if the Harmonor sings the Last Anthem—"

"We must take the chance."

The faint illumination let Allu see the old emissary trembling. "But Allu," he said, "tell me this: how can we fight the Harmonor with such—such *wreckage*?"

"We'll have to find out," she responded.

The commotion behind them increased. A sudden clang rang out loud enough that Allu expected Song Guards to come rushing into the passageway. Voices called out from the shadows:

"Freedom for Siir!"

"Freedom!"

"Down with the Harmonor!"

Ned turned to them. "Hush! Not yet!"

"Freedom *now!*" a woman's voice cried out.

A scattering of notes and chords came forth, echoing.

Allu whispered, "Please, you promised! Wait till the right time!" Then to Sorrik: "I'm afraid we have no choice. Quick, before it gets any lighter." She went ahead, hoping the others would follow her.

Ned came after.

The others did, too.

Although he couldn't see well, Ned could tell they had reached the Great Circle. The outlines of low buildings surrounded them. He remembered this place from countless events: from ceremonies over a period of many years; from his tense conversations with Dessina; from his warm trysts with Allu; and, especially, from the humiliating failure of his avian calliope. Yet despite these memories, so many of them unpleasant, he felt some kind of fire kindle inside him. He followed Allu as she proceeded quickly across the Circle. Looking pleased, she seemed to find what she sought. The curved staircase rose at one end of the Circle, and Allu stopped when she reached it.

Ned saw Sorrik and the prisoners emerge from the fog. A startling sight: all these people appearing as if from nowhere, all those arms and legs, beards and matted hair, torsos and faces. What had been simple turned complex. Grayness turned to color, stillness to motion, silence to sound. Ned heard the chords and notes again, fragments of music as the prisoners approached with the objects they carried.

"Not yet!" Allu whispered.

Most of the prisoners fell silent.

Before anyone could call out, Allu told them, "Here is where we fight the Harmonor. Gather with me here, on the stairs, and face the Harmonor's mountain. Look: the fog is lifting!"

The prisoners obeyed. With much scrambling and scurrying, they all took their places on the curved steps, row after row, with a few stragglers off to each side and with Ned, Allu, and Sorrik standing before them. The noise surprised Ned: sounds like none he had heard before. Bits of melody wafted into the air and dispersed. He tried calling out to the prisoners, pleading with them, urging them to restrain themselves lest the citizens of Sifirithi, the Song Guards, even the Harmonor himself took notice and attacked. Luckily, he assured himself, the city around them remained asleep.

The mist rose then, pulling itself into clouds that obscured the mountains above Sifirithi but left the Square visible. Ned could now see his companions better, and what he saw took his breath away.

The orchestra and the choir put anything in Sifirithi to shame: almost a hundred women, men, and children, shoulder to shoulder, separated only by their instruments—the bells, harps, gongs, pipes, and other fragments of what had once been their cages. What he saw was like the avian calliope, only made of people—a *human* calliope!— something far grander than cages full of birds.

Ned almost cried out in delight. Yet something more than caution restrained him: the expressions on his companions' faces as they glanced about.

Allu noticed too. "What's wrong?" she whispered. "What's the matter?"

Nobody answered. Some of the prisoners began to cry.

Ned, Allu, and Sorrik turned to see what lay behind them.

All around—on staircases, on walls, on rooftops—the people of Sifirithi stood waiting: to the right and left, the Middle and High Choirs; in the center, the Song Guards; and straight ahead, alone, the Harmonor. He gazed right at Allu.

No one spoke. No one moved. The only sound was a faint, uneven tinkling of the Harmonor's crystal chimes.

"So: you have paid me one last visit after all," said the Harmonor. His voice carried clearly through the cold morning air. "I was wondering. You're always late, it seems, but apparently you want to say goodbye before you all vanish forever."

Ned saw that when Allu attempted to reply, no words came forth, not even a whisper. She gestured helplessly.

The Harmonor asked, "Too timid to speak?" He laughed at her.

Ned wanted to shout in fury. Fear restrained him. He looked at Sorrik, pale and trembling. He looked at Allu, distraught and silent.

He glanced at the prisoners clutching their instruments like doomed sailors who cling to floating fragments of their vessel after a shipwreck. He realized just then that their plan was hopeless. Hopeless!

Though Allu's voice sounded no louder than before, she managed to rasp out, "We have come to do musical battle with you."

The Harmonor laughed quietly, as if laughing loudly wouldn't have been worth the trouble. People in the crowd laughed, too, though uneasily.

"We should give up," Sorrik said. "We have already lost."

Some of the prisoners put down the pieces of their musical cages, walked away, entered the stone portal, and disappeared into the mountain.

When the laughter diminished, however, Allu said, "If you are truly the Harmonor, then you are the most powerful music maker in the land. You have nothing to fear from us."

The Harmonor responded, "Even a single Song Guard could crush you—all of you!—like eggshells."

"I'm not talking about Song Guards."

"The Song Guards defend me from all enemies."

"Then you must be helpless without them."

"That's a lie."

"What do you fear, then?" Allu asked. "Fight us yourself."

"Fear?" shouted the Harmonor. "I fear *nothing!*"

"Then do battle with us."

Sorrik cried out, "Allu, please—"

"Do battle with us!"

"Battle?" asked the Harmonor. "You want battle? Don't tempt me."

Allu said, "Do battle with us. We'll see who wins. If you win, you are the greatest music maker in the land. If we win, you can no longer be the Harmonor."

In the stillness following, Ned could hear the Harmonor's crystal pendants clinking. Even those small sounds dizzied him. Only the thought of all those prisoners—and of his parents among them—kept him from panicking. Then, as he waited, the wind picked up, the

Harmonor's glass robe shook, and Ned could feel a torrent of music rush over him like icy rain. At that same moment the sun eased over a distant peak, sunbeams spilled into Sifirithi, and the Harmonor's robe sent needles of light stabbing outward in every direction. People looked away or covered their eyes. Ned winced from the glare.

"Agreed," the Harmonor stated. "We shall see who is the greatest." After a moment's silence, he added, "You may go first."

40

Allu faltered, then turned to her companions. They didn't look impressive now: just a thin old man, a tired boy, and a crowd of sick, exhausted people huddling together. For a moment she felt like surrendering. Instead, she told the prisoners, "Get ready— this is our best chance." And to Ned: "Are you ready?"

"Ready."

Allu and Ned raised their hands, then signalled for everyone to begin.

Ned conducted the human calliope.

Allu conducted the choir.

She tried telling herself that this was the music she hoped for, the music she wanted, the music they all needed. Right away she knew better. Playing fragments of what had been their cages, the harpists plucked their harps. The pipers blew their pipes. The bell-players rang their bells. Everyone played furiously. Allu admired their effort, she found the music powerful and generous, yet she couldn't believe that it would accomplished what they needed.

Ned signaled for the players to fall silent.

The singers continuing singing the song Allu had taught them:

Awake! Awake! Awake, you people!

The choir's melody radiated outward like heat from a hearth, simple and rich, but she wasn't sure that its warmth would be enough to melt the Harmonor's icy heart.

The crowd listened. The Harmonor listened. Allu saw with dismay that the song had no effect on these people.

The choir fell silent. Allu stood gazing at them. A few stared back, clearly as fearful as she herself was; others looked down or looked away. She wanted to call out to them, to thank them for trying, to reassure them, but she couldn't find the words.

At her back, she heard the Harmonor's voice: "A clever tune . . . but not the least bit powerful. Very well—it's my turn."

Allu waited, uncertain.

Some sort of melody arose then, stark as snow sifting out of a winter sky. Allu felt her bones grow cold, as if they were turning into icicles.

> I am your your sleep, your dreams, your rest.
> I am your longings and your pleasure.
> I am the source of humor and of jest.
> I am your gold, your jewels, your treasure.

She listened. She watched the prisoners listening. And the prisoners' instruments collapsed and fell apart: the harp-strings curling like singed hair, the fiddles crumbling into powder.

The Harmonor now sang his terrible refrain:

> I alone can keep you healthy.
> I alone can keep you sane.
> I alone can make you wealthy.
> I alone can ease your pain.

Now the gongs folded and flopped out of the players' hands, the bells melted and streamed to the ground, the flutes dissolved and flowed away. The prisoners cried out in alarm. Some pushed past the others and fled.

> I am your flesh, your bones, your marrow.
> I am your heart, your lungs, your breath.
> I am your veins, both wide and narrow.
> I am the end of suffering and death.

All the drums burst, disintegrated, and sifted down like ashes.

Some of the prisoners turned and ran away.

Sorrik told her, "All is lost. Lost, Allu. Lost."

"Then we are free to do whatever we want," she answered.

"We must surrender."

"Never! We must never submit!"

"We have nothing to play," Sorrik said, gesturing toward the fifty or sixty prisoners who remained.

Allu gazed at them: how they watched, how they wondered, how they waited for the next signal.

The Harmonor's voice came forth: "What are you waiting for? Pick up your instruments and play another tune. I have always wanted to hear someone play dust."

A shivering boy asked, "What are we going to do?"

"Yes, what indeed?" asked an old woman.

Allu said, "We shall sing. Those who have sung before, sing again. Those who have never sung, sing now. Sing with all your might."

"But how?"

"Just sing!" She raised her hands again.

Beginning, the prisoners did exactly what Allu dreaded most: they didn't sing so much as howled, cried, wailed, moaned. Their noises bled together into a terrible clot of sound. Allu herself struggled to resist the urge to plug her ears.

The citizens all around saved her the trouble: their uneasy laughter drowned out the prisoners' din.

Allu glanced at these people angrily. Hadn't Sorrik told her how much everyone hated the Harmonor? She kept wanting them to respond, to take sides. Were they caught up in his power? Were they simply afraid of him? She turned to look at the Harmonor. Even the Harmonor was laughing.

"I have heard dying animals make sweeter sounds," he said.

"Who but the Harmonor would find their death-cries musical?" Allu asked.

There was a brief silence—the deepest, widest silence Allu had heard that morning. Then the Harmonor said, "You are a foolish girl.

Play with fire and you'll burn down the entire house."

"In Sifirithi we could use the heat."

At first the only answer was a tinkle from the Harmonor's robes. Then he said, "You find my city cold? Is that so? We shall see how cold."

The Harmonor now sang a melody like none Allu had heard before, shrill and thin, more a shriek than a tune, as harsh as winter wind against a window. Listening, Allu felt transfixed. It was the starkest, bleakest, emptiest song she had ever heard—the starkest, bleakest, emptiest she could imagine.

> I alone can cure your blindness.
> I alone can shine the light.
> I alone can teach you kindness.
> I alone can say what's right.

Even listening for a few seconds chilled her so deeply that she started shaking. Her teeth rattled. Her hands twitched. Her legs trembled till she could barely stay upright.

Allu realized just then that rain had started falling. Fine mist, then droplets, then heavier drops, then a torrent came down, soaking her. For a moment, she felt a surge of delight: surely this downpour would scatter the citizens, the Song Guards, even the Harmonor. Then she looked around and saw them watching and waiting, everyone still entirely dry. The storm descended only on Allu, Ned, Sorrik, and the prisoners. Soon she couldn't pay attention. Her discomfort grew unbearable. She was on fire from rain so cold that it burned. Allu writhed and twisted. The cold seeped through her skin past her flesh into her bones and lodged there, aching, as if the cold welled up from within. She heard the prisoners crying out, too, helpless to fend off the Harmonor's song.

When she looked up, almost unable to move, Allu discovered that the rain had frozen on the prisoners, on Sorrik, on Ned, and on Allu herself. Ice plated the prisoners' rags and tatters. Ice masked their faces. Ice sheathed their arms, legs, and torsos. Ice clung to their noses, chins, and fingers. They were all trapped: some clad in layers; some shrouded in sheets; some encased within whole mounds like insects in amber. Some of them struggled inside a cage for which icicles formed the bars. Ice bound a boy and girl together so that neither could move without hurting the other. Even those who suffered the least torment couldn't move.

Allu, trapped in ice, found herself paralyzed.

The Harmonor's song had stopped. The only sounds were the prisoners' laments.

The Harmonor called out: "Is that cold enough?"

Allu tried to respond, but her voice had now shrivelled up entirely. Even the merest whisper was impossible.

"What is your answer?" asked the Harmonor. "I hear no words or music. Surely a little sleet won't hold back such a strong young lass."

Once again Allu tried answering. Once again she was mute.

Sorrik, doubled over by the ice, succeeded only in wrenching his head loose. "Allu," he blurted out, "we must surrender. Please! We tried, we did our best, but we've failed. The Harmonor has won."

The Harmonor called out: "Your turn. Or will you relent?"

She was too cold to answer him.

Prisoners called out in despair and pain: "All is lost!"

"We must surrender!"

"The Harmonor will sing the Last Anthem!"

Before Allu could respond, she saw something remarkable. Ned, twisting and turning until fragments of ice cracked off his body and fell to the ground, forced himself free. He stood, staggered forth, and faced the human calliope. All of its players remained stuck in ice. Many were trapped inside cages made of icicles. Stooping, Ned picked up two broken icicles lying on the ground. They must have throbbed painfully in his hands, for he almost dropped them. Yet by force of will he held onto them, raised them, and started to play.

The music was different from what Allu would have expected, the sounds like those made by tapping Lowland pottery rather than Sifir-ithi glass, but it was still music. By tapping against the icicles encasing the prisoners, he brought forth the notes. Long icicles made a deep wooden *thunk;* short ones made a shallower *tink.* Ned took a while figuring out what produced one note or another. Luckily, the prisoners kept still, holding back their shivers and trying not to cry out. Some had fainted. Ned kept playing anyway. Moving this way and that, trying to remember which icicles would bring forth melodies, he played as well as he could, a melody full of warmth despite having its origins in ice.

Ned finished playing.

Some of the people listening laughed at this performance, though Allu was surprised to see many just watching. When she turned to look at the Harmonor, his expression showed nothing but contempt.

"You would play your companions' bones if you had nothing else," he said.

Allu saw Ned hold back his answer.

"You would play their ashes."

Allu herself tried hard to answer but managed only to cough.

"Catching cold?" asked the Harmonor.

Only Allu's anger warmed her.

The Harmonor asked, "Will you surrender?"

Allu shook her head.

Ned said, "Never."

"You must."

Again Allu shook her head. At her back, she heard some of the prisoners moaning and starting to cry.

"Surrender!" cried the Harmonor. "I am the greatest music maker in Sifirithi! In Siir! In the world! Acknowledge me. Obey me. Worship me."

The citizens waited. Nobody moved or made a sound. Even the prisoners at Allu's back fell silent again.

Allu shook her head.

Ned, helpless, stood in silence.

The Harmonor said nothing for a long time. Then his words reached Allu across the Square: "It is my turn now."

41

Ned saw the citizens starting to leave: turning, walking off quickly, easing away from the Great Circle. Their departure terrified Ned more than knowing he had failed, more than hearing the Harmonor's threat. The entire population of Sifirithi had begun to flee. What was about to befall those who remained?

Then the Harmonor sang. Ned tried not to listen, but the anthem gave him no choice. It trapped him. It trapped everyone. He stood there, helpless in the web that tangled him and everyone else.

Much as a rotten log is a tree, the Harmonor's song was music. Much as rust is metal, the Harmonor's song was music. Much as dust is flesh, the Harmonor's song was music. Ned listened in confusion. Dizziness swept through him. His whole body began to feel numb. He wondered what was happening, wondered if it mattered, and ceased to care: a sensation like falling but without the fall. He looked around. Everyone who remained in the Great Circle—the prisoners, the citizens, and the Harmonor—now seemed to grow farther and farther away, though all of them remained right there, motionless. We are frozen, Ned thought. Yet he felt no cold, no pain, only some kind of lightness. He glanced about again, puzzled, almost curious, though not really interested, and he saw all the people fading away. Like snowmen caught in a late winter thaw, everyone twisted and flattened and sank. Even Ned could feel himself collapsing. The hand he held to his face revealed the bones within, yet even the bones were transparent: icicles. Ned thought perhaps he should cry out. He ought to be frightened. Yet nothing startled him now; things simply happened. He wondered for an instant if the rest of Siir, too, would diminish like everything here in Sifirithi. Would Allu disappear? Would his parents dissolve like snow? Would all the people he loved just melt away? It made no difference. Ned didn't care what happened to Allu, to his parents, to Sorrik. He would forget about Sifirithi and the Harmonor and his anthems. He couldn't even think about traitors, prisoners, or the Last Anthem. None of this mattered. Nothing mattered. Siir, Laro, and the whole world would shrink to nothing. And now shrank: for Ned could see the land, the sky, and even his own hands groping around him—everything lighter and lighter, fainter and fainter, smaller and smaller. Soon everything would be nothing.

Then, although he wasn't sure how, Ned heard Allu start to sing. Somehow she had pushed past her silence. She had somehow found her voice. A melody rose from her throat, quiet as blood. Allu sang. Simple and intricate, like spring leaves, the tune unfolded. Puzzling yet clear, the words emerged.

She sang.

42

Allu recognized them at once: the old voices, the night voices, the dream voices. They sang to her. She sang with them, trying hard to stay close to the melody and the words.

Awake, all you people, awake from your slumber!
Why doze through the years of the Harmonor's reign?
Why let this sleep dull you and sadly encumber
The strength to resist this harsh tyrant's disdain?

Think of the wrongs you choose!
Think of the rights you lose!
Think how you wail and cry
As hardships multiply!

Your minds are as keen as the minds of the Masters,
In swiftness and strength you surpass them by far!
Your brave hearts have taught you to weather disasters,
You vastly outnumber your foes in this war!

Why then accept their songs?
Why not resist their wrongs?
What right have they to take
The freedom now at stake?

Awake, friends and loved ones, and sleepwalk no longer—
Rise up and confront this man's hideous powers!
Show him and his minions which side is the stronger
When we, the Realm's people, take back what is ours!

As she sang, Allu felt herself growing solid again—her bones
strong, her flesh warm—and she could see the people around her
taking shape again, turning substantial: eyes watching her. Sifirithi
rushed at her from all sides.

She wasn't afraid. The voices stayed with her, and Allu sang with
them.

Then silence—

Allu didn't know where she was—or *what* she was. Dead? Asleep?

She forced herself to look up. Ned gazed down at her. Sorrik too.
Some of the prisoners huddled around her. Others as well: some of
the citizens.

Ned stroked the hair out of Allu's face with warm, soft hands.

When Allu tried speaking, her throat seared as if from swallowing
embers. She could barely whisper even a single word: "Where—?"

Sorrik and Ned helped her sit. She was astonished to find herself
on the ground. The Great Circle, Sifirithi, and the mountains rose
around her. Allu glanced about, dazed. Hundreds of people stood
nearby. The intensity of their expressions frightened her at first; then
she saw that there was no contempt in those faces, no anger, no hate.

All the ice was gone, but the Harmonor remained. Smiling calmly,
he spoke to the nearest squad of Song Guards: "Take her back into
the mountain."

Allu felt her flesh grow cold. Her song had failed. She had failed.
She gazed at Ned in despair.

But then Allu saw something take place that she never could have
imagined. People didn't obey the Harmonor. The Song Guards

glanced at one another but made no move to follow the Harmonor's command. Some people even laughed and jeered at him.

Hearing the laughter and the jeers, the Harmonor lashed out: "How dare you! Shall I sing again?"

"Sing anything you like!" someone shouted.

"We don't care what you sing!" called out another.

The Harmonor's face tightened. He pointed to several more squads of Song Guards. "You: capture them! You as well: restrain them with an anthem."

Once again the Song Guards ignored him—not just these squads but others present.

"Did you hear me?" asked the Harmonor. *"Capture them!"*

Allu watched in astonishment as several of the squads not only disobeyed the Harmonor but mobilized, turned on him, and captured him instead.

"Stop at once!" he shouted, his crystal pendants clinking and clanking. "Release me!"

The Song Guards did nothing of the kind. They bundled the Harmonor in a cloak like spiders wrapping a fly in their silky web, then carried him off toward the mountain's portal.

No one among the hundreds present moved to intervene.

What happened next surprised Allu even more than what had just taken place.

People left. First a few, then small clusters, then large groups of people simply left. Squads of Song Guards, the several choirs, and the gathered citizens of Sifirithi simply turned and walked off.

A thin woman—one of the prisoners—now turned to Allu: "You have freed us."

Another woman shouted, "You have freed Sifirithi and Siir!"

A man standing nearby proclaimed, "You are the new Harmonor!"

"Never!" Allu whispered, rejecting these words as if spitting out poison someone had forced her to drink. Almost at once she lost her balance. She would have fallen if Ned and Sorrik hadn't supported her.

Someone called out: "Teach us your song!"

Someone else: "You are the new Harmonor!"

"Never!" she told them, staggering away. *"Never!"*

Ned and Sorrik supported her as Allu walked off. She felt so weak that she almost collapsed. When they reached the place where the Harmonor had stood, they turned and looked around.

The Great Circle was almost empty.

Allu forced herself to speak again: "There will never be a Harmonor—ever! There will never be music like the Harmonor's."

"Teach us your song!" someone shouted.

Allu shook her head. Even whispering was difficult now. She struggled to respond. "I would teach it," she told them, faltering, almost unable to continue—"if you needed it."

Then her voice fell silent.

EPILOGUE

My name is Sorrik. Once I was Sorrik-koru, First-Order Emissary to the Lowlands. Now I am just Sorrik. Once I spent my time finding young people to transport for proper training as singers in Sifirithi. Now I live in the Lowland myself, where I listen to any and all who wish to sing. Once I was an old man. Now I am a very old man whose life will soon be over, yet I feel complete, happy, and at peace.

When I first met Allu, I told her that I never sing. That statement was the truth. I didn't sing then, nor do I now. Singing has never been among my abilities. I do tell tales, however, which are songs in their own way. For this reason I have told you my tale about a lass who sang and a lad who built instruments. Why? Because it needed telling. Like Allu's dreamsongs, which often welled up and demanded to be sung, this tale demanded to be told.

I'm not altogether finished, however, so listen to me just a short while longer.

What's most important is that everyone abandoned the great mountain city and went back to the Lowland. (Almost everyone. I'll explain that word "almost" in a moment.) The denizens of Sifirithi simply left. Once they realized that they needn't stay, they didn't. Some departed in sleighs. Many dressed in warm clothes, loaded a few possessions on their backs, and walked out. By following the paths that the runners and the sleighs had cut into the snowy landscape, all of these people descended into the Lowland. Then they dispersed. In this way almost the entire populace of Sifirithi abandoned the city that had once held sway over the Realm of Siir.

And that realm? I'll tell you more about Siir in a moment.

But regarding Allu . . . She arrived in Laro a few days after the strange final events in Sifirithi. Once she finished greeting the villagers and made her way through the town's winding streets—streets that seemed at once unfamiliar and strangely new—Allu reached her own house. She hesitated for a moment, then opened the door and stepped inside.

Her family, seated at the kitchen table, looked up in surprise as she entered.

Allu shut the door behind her.

No one spoke. Everyone just stared. Allu saw at once how frightened they were—Mother holding her spoon in midair, as if frozen; Father staring at her in alarm; her brother and her sisters glancing at Allu, then at each other, then at Allu again.

In a hoarse voice she said, "I'm back."

No one said anything for a long time. Then her mother said, "We know . . . what you did."

"I did what I needed to do."

"Now surely you'll do the same," her father said.

Puzzled, Allu asked, "Do the same? What do you mean?"

She noticed one of her sisters starting to weep.

Her father continued: "You'll sing another of your lullabies, won't you? We saw what those lullabies can do. You'll sing us to sleep, just as you sang so many people here to sleep."

Allu shook her head. "No, not at all. I won't. I wouldn't. I don't sing like that now. I can't sing at all."

"Not at all?"

"I can hardly talk."

Even as she spoke, Allu's voice faded to a whisper.

Her family watched her, waiting. When a log in the hearth popped, everyone jolted, but otherwise no one moved or made a sound.

Then Allu's father asked, "So what will you do?"

"I thought," Allu replied, "perhaps I'll sit with you now. To be with you. To be home again."

≈ ≈ ≈

And Ned?

I'm delighted to say that Ned, like Allu, returned to the Lowland. At first he spent his time in Ftora, his home town, where he helped his parents settle in again following their long imprisonment. They had been separated for so many years that both he and his parents wanted time together. And so they spent several weeks together, told stories about what had befallen them over the years, and delighted in one another's company after such a cruel time apart. After a while, however, Ned traveled to another town and attended to another matter looming large in his mind.

He found Allu working in her family's workshop. Standing near the forge, she happened to be pounding a radiant iron bar with a big hammer as he entered. The metal rang out, bell-like, with each blow. So intent was Allu on her work that she didn't even notice Ned come in. Her parents did, however, as they worked nearby. To Ned's surprise, they smiled at him, each nodding once, and then stepped outside. *They know who I am,* he thought—*and perhaps they even know why I'm here.*

At this point Allu caught sight of him. The hammer hung in the air for a moment. Then she lowered it, set aside the glowing bar, and turned to face him.

They hesitated for a moment, smiling, before they walked closer and embraced.

"I am here, you are there," she whispered, "and now we stand—"

"No," Ned told her warmly. "*I* am here. *You* are here. And *here* we stand."

In this way Allu and Ned were united once again.

I'm happy to tell you that within a short while the town of Laro celebrated this couple's wedding—a wedding filled with all the music that people there could muster, music that they scarcely knew how to sing or play, yet music rich with everyone's joy and hope. Musicians played instruments, singers sang ballads, choirs sang songs, storytellers told stories, and everyone present—Allu and Ned, Allu's family, Ned's parents, and hundreds of villagers—danced till dawn.

What about the Harmonor?

I wish I could report that following his humiliating defeat, this sad, lonely man fled from Siir and never came back. I regret to tell you that he didn't flee. He did, however, do what became the next best thing for everyone else in Siir: he remained in Sifirithi even though almost everyone else had left. To this day the Harmonor lives in his glass palace listening to the clink and clank of the myriad crystal chimes he wears—the only music that interests him. A handful of servants wait on him as if that ice-hearted man were somehow still the king of a great realm. The regrettable truth is that some people will follow even the most foolish of tyrants. Worse yet, some tyrants linger even when they lose their power. What I find reassuring is that the Harmonor rules over an empty, cold city—and nowhere else.

Life elsewhere in Siir was anything but empty. Life was *full*. Life—and music, which are two forms of the same thing.

Old people who had sung songs long ago now worked hard to remember them: putting the tunes and the words back together, teaching what they knew to anyone who asked. Young people learned songs from other people but also made up and sang their own. Craftsmen returned to building lutes and fiddles, flutes and horns, bells and gongs and drums, harps of many kinds, and instruments that no one had ever played before. Minstrels showed up from distant lands to sing and play their ballads, airs, and tunes. Crowds gathered to hear all of these musicians.

Allu never sang again, but everyone else did. She, like everyone else, went to hear these people. She and Ned lived in Laro but traveled throughout the realm, and everywhere they went the people treated them with love and respect. Each town celebrated their presence. Village singers often bade them come and hear the music they themselves performed. Allu and Ned delighted in everyone's music. Allu felt pleased, too, when people sang the music she now composed—music that stayed silent within her but emerged through other people's voices. Ned enjoyed the music that people performed on instruments they themselves had invented.

Now my song, as I've called it, is sung.

And yours? I hope you sing, too, proudly and fearlessly, each of you in your own voice.

ABOUT THE AUTHOR

Born in Denver and raised in Colorado, Mexico, and Peru, E. J. Myers attended Grinnell College and the University of Denver. He has worked in a wide variety of professions and trades, including inpatient health care, emergency medical services, carpentry, cabinetmaking, and publishing. He is the author of forty-two published books, most issued by mainstream companies, among them four novels (*The Mountain Made of Light, Fire and Ice, The Summit,* and *Last Things*); fourteen children's books; and a well-received, much-reprinted book about bereavement, *When Parents Die: A Guide for Adults.* His recent *On Whitcomb Hill: Land, House, and History in Rural Vermont,* received high praise from *Vermont History.* Among his publications are over a dozen books that Myers co-authored or ghostwrote for clients and other authors. He lives with his wife in central Vermont.

For information about E. J. Myers, visit his Web site at:

www.edwardmyerswriter.net

ABOUT MONTEMAYOR PRESS

Montemayor Press is an independent publisher of literature for
adults and children. To learn more about our books, visit:

www.MontemayorPress.com

or write for a catalogue at:

Montemayor Press
P. O. Box 546
Montpelier, VT 05601